Shell Castle

Mark Raney

ISBN: 978-0-578-02855-2

TO: MADELINE

CHAPTER ONE

We work in a fishery that is dying, and in several years we will no longer be able to make our living as commercial clammers. These are the truths that are clearly ahead of us. But since they are painful to accept, we avoid talking about them as much as possible. Sometimes we talk about them as though they are happening to clammers in other parts of eastern North Carolina. Other times we change the subject when they come up in conversation. But still they remain the truths that we will finally have to accept one day soon.

This is another example of man overwhelming natural resources with tools and with crowds and with tenacity. The clam resources probably could withstand the tools and the tenacity for years to come because it is bountiful and it recovers quickly. But it cannot withstand the endless crowds that are out harvesting clams everyday. So the resource is greatly reduced now, and next year it will be further reduced, and the next year and the next with no end in sight to the crowds. And we can only continue to work in this fishery of ours that is dying.

Because we love to make our living in open skiffs on the coastal sounds and in the bays and rivers and creeks as commercial clammers through summer and fall and winter and spring and summer again and again. But when the resource does become so depleted that we can no longer make our living at it, then we will be forced to stop. But none of us will stop until all of us are forced to stop. Because several stopping will not give the resource much relief. Because there are many others coming into it to more than take the place of the few who might stop. And each year more and more of the available bottom becomes closed either temporarily or permanently because of pollution. So we truly do work in a fishery that is dying. But still we choose not to accept that truth. And instead it has become a great personal dread that we hold close inside that has become quite tender. Because we are very proud of who we are and what we do and where we do it. But in our hearts way past our selfishness, none of us are proud of how much we could do to conserve the resource while instead doing nothing.

Because commercial fishermen of every type fish. We fish and fish, and we will not stop fishing until there is either so little left to catch that it is not worthwhile going any longer, or someone comes along and forces us to stop. But we never stop fishing freely on our own from wisdom. Because that is the way we have always been, and that is the way we always will be. And this clam resource here is certainly not the first fishery that we have so thoroughly depleted, and it will not be the last fishery that we so thoroughly deplete. And the bureaucrats here will not force us to stop because to do so they would have to stick their necks out and do something that would be unpopular with the local voters. Because bureaucrats simply do not stick their necks out and be unpopular with voters. And that is the way they have always been, and that is the way they always will be. Besides, with the clam resource here dead finally, it will take four times as many bureaucrats to step in and rebuild the clam populations and habitats to somewhere near their original state. So we can only continue to live with the personal dread of working in a dying fishery that we are killing. But usually it just feels as though we are merely playing out a grand plan that others somewhere have carefully made without our knowledge.

Then once again July then August staggers us with their relentless sun until our eyes are badly red streaked and itchy and our already too tanned skin is further burned until it tingles and swells and cracks and hurts. With mornings of no wind and oppressive humidity until we feel dizzyingly sick. Then afternoons of piling high billows of building thunderstorms that release themselves in sheet after sheet of wind driven hard cold rain with lightning flashes that blind and thunder concussions that deafen and again and again. And we are very proud of our relentless stamina also.

CHAPTER TWO

"You're a salty son of a bitch if you clammed through that storm, " Wormshoe says from behind the bar as he reaches for a beer in the cooler.

"Just a summer sprinkle, Wormshoe, good for the roses, " I say smiling, sitting on a stool as my eyes adjust to the inside dimness after the late afternoon glare now that the thunderstorm has passed.

"How'd you do?" Larry asks from the next stool. His forearms leaning against the bar, a hard flat hand slowly turning his beer in the wet rings it makes.

"Hello Larry, didn't see you. Five hundred."

"Not bad, I only got two seventy five. Motor trouble again. I think it's the carburetor." But Larry is scared of lightning so he always runs before storms then makes up other reasons for stopping clamming early. Which no one would blame him if he just admitted that lightning scares the hell out of him, but he won't. Because you have to be a hungry clammer to stay out on the water in an open skiff in a big wide bay through a summer thunderstorm. "You didn't stay through the storm did you?"

"Yeah, through most of it. I ran to the leaning water oak where the bank is washed out when it really got bad." But Larry and I have had this conversation before and it always leads to the same place. And I have already set myself up to have the conversation again.

"Worse place you can get, under a tree. They're nothing but lightning rods."

"Well, I didn't want to come in early."

"Friend of mine in Long Island got struck doing that. Killed him dead as a mackerel. Nothing but charred meat. A few clams more just ain't worth it, I always say."

'Screw what you say and you and Long Island and your Long Island friend too,' I think. I never learn. Larry knows everything, and you can't tell him anything, and every conversation with him ends in an argument. And I never learn to just agree with him, then ignore him.

"There's a million trees out there, Larry. I was under only one." No, I never learn. I must enjoy arguing with brick walls.

"One is all it takes, the wrong one. You'll wise up when you've been working the water as long as I have."

"So you're the wise old man of the water, huh? The know everything about everything." Now I am suddenly pissed. I had come in in a good mood, now I am pissed.

"I know what I know." Nodding wisely to himself.

"Well, piss on what you know. How'd you find your drunk ass way down here from Long Island anyway?" With Larry still leaning against the bar slowly turning his beer, and still nodding wisely to himself. But usually we are friends and get along, that is until he starts the, "I know what I know," shit. And he is a good clammer when there aren't so many storms to run in from. And he could be a better clammer if he would ease up some on the beer. Because you can work, or you can drink. But if you keep drinking while you work, the work will eventually go to hell. But that is Larry's business. And I am usually very good about minding my own business. That is until Larry gets me pissed, which he can easily do. But five hundred clams isn't a bad day for around Swansboro now. It isn't anything like it use to be around here when a thousand clam day was usual. But five hundred at ten cents each is a fifty dollar bill day. And I feel good about that and about staying through the storm and not coming in early.

"You'll wise up when you've been working the water as long as I have," he says like a broken record repeating itself.

But I shut my mouth. And I keep telling myself to keep it shut and to just ignore him. Because now that my eyes have adjusted to the dimness, I see that Larry is pretty well sloshed. He probably has been sitting on that stool most of the afternoon swilling beer as long as it took for the thunderstorm to build before it broke. So now he is in a broken record drunk mood. But I have my good mood back now, and I decide to not lose it again in a senseless argument with Larry. So I look down the bar to see if Carl has come in yet. "Hey Wormshoe, has Carl come in yet?"

"Haven't seen him," Wormshoe says in between talking with a shrimper down the bar. Wormshoe had worked the stern deck of Sammy's trawler for years before Sammy lost it for running marijuana. How they didn't serve any time and how Sammy bought this bar, after getting caught with a boatload of marijuana, no one knows. And we don't want to know either. Because we know what's good for us. But it had to take a lot of pull from someone who had a lot of pull that he wasn't using right then. But Wormshoe got his nickname honestly. Because a wormshoe is a two by four or six or eight of cheap soft pine that is nailed to the keel of a wood boat so the marine boreworms can get into it long before they start to get into the good bottom lumber. So a wormshoe is expendable and it is sacrificed. And Wormshoe has always been Sammy's wormshoe for whatever business Sammy happens to be in at the time. And particularly so now with this bar that fronts, for God knows what, that goes on in back, that we don't want to know about either. And since Wormshoe is thick and squat and powerfully built, we are always real friendly toward him. And since he loves what he does for Sammy and since he is very good at what he does also, we always tip him well. Because we don't know, but one day one of us might have a desperate need of some of the heavy pull that Sammy has ready access to.

So I motion to Wormshoe to bring me another beer, and one for Larry also. Then I hear Larry start to tell the guy next to him about his carburetor trouble. Next will be trees and lightning and his charred meat Long Island friend. Yeah, liking Larry today will be too much work. So I look at myself in the wide mirror that is behind the bar, and I am again startled at how deeply tanned I am. With my sharp nose and high cheek bones, I look like an Indian that has been much too long under a burning desert sun. You can see white when I smile or when I relax the squint wrinkles around my eyes, other than that I am not easily seen here in the dimness though I am sitting right out in the middle of everyone. The newly tanned tourists who are everywhere around here now look more healthy with their tans and have a good glow about them. But I just look painfully burnt and passed dried out and into leathery. Then I see Carl in the mirror coming in, his eyes still squinted from the glare. "There you are," I say so he would know that it is me here in the dimness, "didn't know if you would stop by today."

"Stayed for another hundred."

"How'd you do?"

"Seven fifty."

"Not bad, fella, not bad at all."

"There's no end to the Doctor bills."

"How's Jamie doing?"

"Another operation this winter and his foot should be pretty well straightened out."

"It's been rough for the little fella."

"Yeah, but it's better to get it done now while he's so young."

"How'd you do?" Larry leans forward and asks Carl. Then right away he starts into the carburetor trouble, trees, lightning and his charred meat Long Island friend shit before Carl can answer. All of it but the real reason he came in early. So I sit here between them holding my breath, because Carl doesn't even try to like Larry and he isn't subtle about his dislike either. And you can't really blame Carl because he does have a lot on his mind what with

Jamie's foot and the Doctor bills and everything. And, too, Carl has never had much patience with people who are full of shit, like Larry is usually full of shit. But mostly it is because while Carl drinks and now and then drinks too much, he doesn't have any use what so ever for drunks, and especially for drunks that work the water. Carl says that they give the rest of us a bad name. And he is right there. Because the tourists have long thought that all of fishermen are nothing but a bunch of drunks. Oh, they flock here to the coast for our fresh seafood and they rave about it while eating it and they go back home and urge their neighbors to hurry and come down here and have some, but all the while they are thinking that we fishermen who provide it are nothing but a bunch of drunks. It's like going to Texas for great steaks while assuming that all cowboys are nothing but a bunch of bums. Of course cowboys don't have much to do with beef anymore, while we fishermen still have everything to do with seafood. But I really don't understand why the tourists feel about us the way they do. But at the same time, neither do I let it bother me very much. Because I have pretty well stopped caring what other people think of me, and I have started to live my life more for myself and what I think of myself now. But Carl still cares and it bothers him some now and then, so he isn't all subtle about his dislike for Larry. So I sit here between them and hold my breath, while fully expecting Carl to reach across in front of me and knock Larry's drunk ass off the stool.

But Carl and I have always gotten along well together. Most days we finish our clamming day some where near each other.

Then we run in with our skiffs abreast and holler back and forth about our day and the weather and the tide and this and that. Carl is almost always top clammer around here because he works harder than the rests of us. I mean you can just see the harder concentration and the more determination in his face while he is clamming. And all of us accept Carl as top clammer because he has earned it. And I have learned a lot about clamming from him. But then, ever since I started fishing, I have made it a point to always work near fishermen who are very good at whatever fishery we are working at the time. Fishermen who take commercial fishing really seriously as their profession. For example, during the winter bay scallop season of Mondays and Wednesdays, I scallop with or near David Willis because David is almost always top scalloper. He has a full-time job inland, but his home is here and his father was a fisherman and his father also. But David isn't a full-time fisherman like they had been and like we are. But he takes his vacation leave and most of his sick leave during the scallop season because he truly loves to scallop and for those two days a week he takes it seriously as a profession. So from the first I have made it a point to fish near the really good fishermen, so I can learn from them. Because there aren't any how to books on how to be a commercial fisherman, so like everyone else I have had to learn by trial and error and from those who are really good. That is how it was when I started clamming. I stumbled around a lot like any other drylander trying to learn this totally different type of work in this totally different world of working the water. After watching Carl from afar for weeks and into months, he finally gradually took me under his wing and taught me how to do the fundamentals the right way and then later some of the more complicated techniques and then I was on my own. And I still appreciate Carl's doing that. So, yeah, we do get along well together. And as determined as I am, he is a more determined clammer. But then he has a wife and a kid with a club foot so he has more reasons to be more determined.. But then Carl is more determined about everything, that's just the kind of fella he is, so he probably would be a more determined clammer than I am even without the wife and the kid with the club foot. And he is a stronger clammer than I am because he is built stronger. But you don't notice Carl's strong build right away the way you notice Wormshoe's powerful build right away. But I am teaching myself to be a smarter clammer. And I have come a long way, and I am getting there quickly, and Carl knows it. And when I am there finally, then my smarter clamming will equal his stronger clamming. But Carl doesn't mind the competition because it just makes him even more determined.

But to be a good fisherman in whatever fishery, that's the way you have to do it. Because you have to be resourceful and you have to be self- sufficient, and you have to keep your eyes and ears open and always be learning how to do things better and simpler and faster. You begin with the abilities that you have, then keep improving those while developing more abilities. It is exciting and never ending. It is fascinating and I truly love it. And it is the most basic and the most honest work I have ever done. With clamming for example, how much money you earn for a day is determined entirely by how hard you work and how long you work and how smart you work. Bring in a hundred clams at ten cents each and you make a ten dollar bill. Bring in a thousand clams at ten cents each and you make a hundred dollar bill. See, it's entirely up to you. It isn't like an inland job where most of the time you can hide from the boss in a crowd and wait for the time clock to do it's work. Out here the kind of a man you are quickly becomes obvious to everyone. Because there are always more reasons why you don't have to work, than there are reasons for you to work. That is why you have a Larry at one end of the yardstick, and a Carl at the other end of the yardstick. Because Carl always manages to make at least a decent days' pay in spite of anything and everything. And I am close behind him and closing fast.

So I am still sitting here holding my breath. But Carl doesn't reach across in front of me and knock Larry's drunk ass off the stool. He just keeps looking at Larry with those dull cold eyes that he gets when he's pissed, with his mouth white pressed shut, then finally Larry finishes his bullshit story and is back nodding wisely at the beer he slowly turns. So I breathe a quiet sign of relief because we are all in this together and we should at least try to get along.

So to change the subject, I say, "Carl, I've been thinking that it's about Ocracoke time again." But Ocracoke is the reason I had stopped by Sammys's today looking for Carl.

Right away his eyes clear and his mouth relaxes, and he says, "yeah, I've been thinking about Ocracoke a lot lately too."

"So let's see if we can get up a trip to there next week."

"Sounds good to me, Keith."

Because every summer about this time we begin to get restless. It probably is the everyday sameness of the heat and the humidity and the glare. And the everyday late afternoon thunderstorms, and the every day clamming the same areas. But every summer about this time we begin thinking Ocracoke, or at least we have for the past several summers.

Because in spring, after the late winter northeasters one after the other after the other, the water quality along the coast improves enough so the Marine Fisheries people temporarily open previously closed areas to clamming around Southport, or behind Topsail Island and into New River, or up around Morehead City and Beaufort and towards Harkers Island. So we haul out our skiffs and go clam those areas. And since the areas haven't been clammed for a year or longer, then for several days we make much better than average money. Of course there is the added expenses of travel and ramp fees and docking fees and motel rooms if it is too far to go and come in a day, and eating in restaurants always costs more. But usually the added income more than makes up for these expenses. And the change in scenery is good, and the change in routine is good. Then we come back to clam here around Swansboro, for the remainder of spring and well into summer. Until just about now.

"Larry, Carl and I are thinking about going to Ocracoke, want to go?" And as soon as I start saying that, I can't believe that I am saying that. I can't believe that I haven't let this sleeping dog lie. What is it about me that makes me want all this here to be like we all are at camp and sitting around a roaring bonfire in the evening singing songs?

"The grass is always greener."

"What kind of an answer is that?"

"That's my answer."

"You want to go or not?"

"A bird in the hand."

And Carl is looking at me in incredible wonderment for starting this conversation when I certainly know better. But I am already into it now.

"And faint heart never wins fair lady, whatever the hell that means. You want to go or not?"

"I'll think about it."

"Don't do me any favors. Just thought I'd ask."

"I'll let you know."

"Larry, I don't give a good goddamn whether you go or not! Just thought I'd ask!" And I can hear me hollering to myself, 'shut your mouth, fool, will you just shut your mouth!'

"I said I'd let you know."

Now my mouth is pressed white shut again, and Carl is still shaking his head in incredible wonderment. Then he motions to Wormshoe for another round of beer.

Because saltwater is corrosive to everything down here whether wood or metal or man. It is the complete freedom to go to work if you want to and to go to work when you want to. The freedom to stop early or to stay late. The freedom to drag ass through the work or to bust ass to do more work and to do it better. The key is to set an overall goal for the day, then to break up that overall goal into hourly goals which you attain one by one just for yourself. And I have learned to handle this complete freedom better now than when I began working the water five years ago. But the temptation to ease up and to cut short and to get by is always present to be fought against. Because saltwater really can corrode you and turn you worthless, just as it does everything else down here.

Then Tom comes in. So Carl asks him if he wants to go to Ocracoke. And Tom says that he sure needs to for the money, but that he is building a skiff for a tourist and had better stay and finish it. Tom is teaching himself to be a boat builder for when the clamming dies finally. Because the tourists can buy new skiffs, even if we fishermen cannot, because the tourists always have plenty of money for messing around on the water. Fishermen have a special respect for boat builders, just as we have a special respect for the Coast Guard. Our lives are in the hands of the boat builders everyday in quiet ways. But our lives can suddenly come in the hands of the Coast Guard on those few days when everything that can go wrong does go wrong, and try as we may we cannot reverse them. So you can feel the more respect that Tom has been getting lately. He feels it also, and we can see it in the more care that he gives to the skiffs that he is building.

We work one man to a skiff around here, unless a fella's outboard is in the shop and he needs a ride in and out. When we work the temporary openings at Beaufort or Southport or wherever, we work two men to a skiff to cut down on expenses. But for Ocracoke we work two teams of two men to a skiff. To cut down on expenses, yes, because we also pool food costs for there, but more for the safety of a backup skiff and outboard and two other fellas just in case. Because going to Ocracoke is a whole hell of a lot further than just going down the road aways around here. Because Ocracoke then Portsmouth Island are the barrier island that enclose to the east that huge area that is Pamlico Sound and south of there, Core Sound. And to get to there from here, we have to go past Morehead City then Beaufort, then hang a hard right east past Williston, then more northeast past Davis and Stacy and Sealevel and Atlantic to get to the ferry landing at Cedar Island for the two and a half hour run out to Ocracoke. When we say we are going to Ocracoke to clam, what we really mean is that we are going through Ocracoke to get to Shell Castle to clam. We leave the ferry at its Ocracoke landing, go around the harbor to the public boat ramp, launch our skiffs and run out of the harbor due south across Ocracoke Inlet for five miles to get to the several clustered shelly marsh islands that combined are called Shell Castle. The open water of the Inlet then the sprawling Atlantic are eastward, and the open water of the huge Pamlico Sound is westward. The barrier island of Portsmouth is southeast and it runs slow and lazy southward to the far distance where Core Sound is.

So with the day that it takes to get to Shell Castle, and the day that it takes to get back, and the several days of clamming and camping out on marsh islands, this is a trip that we plan as carefully as possible. Because, as the old salts around here say, 'if you're man enough to take a skiff away from the dock, you damn well better be man enough to bring it back.' But it is because of Shell Castles's isolation that the clams there are still concentrated enough so we can each make two to three hundred dollars a day with a hard days work. And it is this that makes going there well worth the time and the trouble and the expense. But going to Shell Castle is a real adventure also. And the best part of being a commercial clammer is the simple adventure of it all.

Then Larry nudges me and says that he is going home, and that he will see me later. And I say, yeah, okay, later Larry. But when he is at the door two crabbers are coming in and I hear him start into them about his carburetor, and I already know where that is going. So Carl says that Larry sure can be a pain in the ass. And I agree, but say that I can't help but like him. But Carl just shakes his head to that.

Sammy's is about full of late afternoon fishermen now. Clammers and crabbers in for several beers after our work day. Ocean trawler shrimpers in between trips. Flounder giggers and bay shrimpers and gillnetters in for several beers before their work night. Yeah, the pressure that all of us put on the resources here is relentless and massive all right. But by seven or eight o'clock all of us fishermen will be gone. Then Sammy's will begin to fill with full time day jobbers. And the smell in here will go from sweat and saltwater to soap and after shave. And the conversations up and down the bar will go from all about work to anything but work.   But Wormshoe adjusts to this male tide change smoothly and easily and even handedly towards all. Sometimes we in the day crowd get hot headed during our winding down. And sometimes those in the night crowd get frenzied in their getting wound up. But so far no one in either crowd has been foolish enough to see if Wormshoe really is expendable. And whatever Sammy has going on in back, that Wormshoe fronts for, goes on there with the night crowd. But as I said, we in the day crowd don't want to know about that. And you rarely see a tourist here in Sammy's day or night. Just as you rarely see one of us in their Lounges. Now and then I go to a Lounge with Jennifer when she is down from Greensboro for a weekend before we go to a restaurant to eat. But I do not feel comfortable in those places now that I am a fisherman. And now and then when she is down Jennifer comes with me here to Sammy's in the late afternoon. But she feels comfortable anywhere and anytime and with any crowd. And she is a damn fine looking woman. And the other fishermen make silly fools of themselves with their bragging and showing off when she is here. And she really enjoys that. And I am always as proud of being with Jennifer as I would be of having a three thousand clam day.

But by now Carl and I have just about run out of names of good clammers to go with us to Ocracoke. One of us know a reason why this fella or that fella can't go or won't go. Because camping out on a marsh island for four nights and three days isn't for everyone. It means no shower and no shave for that time. It means going to the toilet in the marsh grass. And the dried saltwater begins to cake and the sand begins to chafe and our smell quickly gets rank. It means cooking on an unfamiliar camp stove, and the pots and pans never really get clean with just sand and saltwater to clean them with. And since the ice melts after the first day, several days of warm beer and soda and canned food rather than fresh meat. And sleeping on an air mattress that somehow always gets punctured the first night by marsh grass stubble. And since there isn't anything else to do and no where else to go, it means hard clamming for ten to twelve hours a day rather than the usual six to eight hours around here. But to bring back six or seven hundred dollars worth of clams after expenses, some of us will go anywhere and put up with anything.

Then after a silence, Carl says, "well, there's always Charlie and Jack."

"Yeah, but I was hoping we could think of two fellas who get along better."

"I don't know why those two can't get along. Separate, they're not bad fellas, together, and the sparks fly."

"And they don't keep their gear in good shape."

"But it's their gear, they have to use it. Our gear is always first class."

"Yeah." But I am still hesitant, still hoping we can think of two other fellas.

"So we find Charlie and Jack between now and tomorrow, and we all meet here tomorrow afternoon to plan the trip."

"Yeah.   Okay," still racking my brain without success, "maybe they'll get along better this trip."

"Maybe, but don't count on it." Carl says already resigned to Charlie and Jack for better or worse.

"Yeah, you're right," me trying not to let the trip get spoiled and it hasn't even started yet, "ready for a beer?"

"One more," Carl says looking at his watch, "then Sara will have supper ready."

So I sit here still hoping that we can think of two other fellas before tomorrow afternoon.   Because from Ocracoke to Shell Castle to Portsmouth Island and south to Core Sound is special to me. And from one trip to the next I can see it exact and shining in my mind. And I can feel the thousand years of its evolution. And I don't want this trip spoiled.

I had been other types of workman before I became a fisherman. And I was skilled at those types of work just as now I am skilled at fishing. But those types of work always brought with them a bossman and set hours and a list of dos and don'ts. So gradually I decided that I was tired of always having someone telling me what to do and when to do it. So I came here and became a tougher bossman on myself than any previous bossman had been. And I work longer and harder than before. And I am very serious about my own list of dos and don'ts. And I go looking for gear of mine to clean or repair or to replace. But then working where we do you better become this way. Because commercial fishing is dangerous work. Because just being in a skiff on the water is dangerous. And add to that, being in a skiff on the water almost everyday fall to winter to spring to summer to fall again. And add to that, constantly changing weather and tides and wind. And add to that, always moving around in a small area that is always wet and shifting and bouncing. Because things break and things slip and things wear out and things fall. So cuts and scrapes and bruises are common out here. And busted legs and backs and heads are usual out here. And death is not really that rare either.

CHAPTER THREE

Something is forcing me to come back from that warm blurry nothingness that is so far away. But staying there lost and gone dreaming is all that matters. So I begin to get irritable in protest. Then I hear, "Keith," and know that this isn't for the first time, but it still sounds all echoy like it is coming from down a long tunnel. But I can feel myself coming back quickly now in spite of the protest. I am sleeping on my stomach with my head to one side, my nose and the side of my face all scrunched into the pillow. "Hhunhhh?" I ask irritably at this rudeness.

"Keith, wake up so we can talk." The sexy low huskiness is still in Jennifer's voice.

"Hhunhhh?" I ask again in protest. But I have been forced to almost fully back now. Then her cool hand is on my shoulder nudging me into all the way back.

"God, you're so hot, and you're even more tanned."

"I'm burnt. My skin hurts," I say into the pillow.

"You look deliciously well done," she laughs. Then she leans down and kisses my shoulder, and her lips are soft and cool and moist. And her black black hair falls across my face and it is cool also, and once again I smell the perfume that is hers alone. Then she leans up, there sitting on the side of the bed smiling down at me.

"Didn't think you were coming until tomorrow." My eyes blink and try to focus with the hall light so bright. But my irritable protest is fully gone now because my Jennifer is here again finally.

"Robert has a closing tomorrow on a condo out at The Waves. We came down to take the client and his wife out to eat tonight."

I always flinch inwardly when her husbands' name is mentioned. But this is more from jealousy than from guilt. Because he can be with her anytime, or he can be with her all the time. But I am rarely with Jennifer, and I never know when the next time will be. And their marriage seems like a business arrangement to me rather than a love contract. And he is so controlled in speech and dress and mannerisms that he seems packaged like you can go to a store and buy any one of a thousand exactly like him. So I find it difficult to take Robert seriously. I mean really, his being a Lawyer to only the rich and his never dealing with crime and criminals always seems like it is too easy and too safe. At least if he was a real man, a man's man. And their world is a world I have never known and a world I will never know. But it is also a world that I really don't want to know. But yeah, there is a lot of raw jealousy when I think of Robert.

So I roll over onto my back, and now her hand is rubbing my chest. Her eyes bright smiling down at me, the hall light haloing her black black hair so it shimmers. So I fall in love with Jennifer all over again.

"Your chest is still very sexy." And her perfume is

everywhere in the bedroom now like it has taken possession.

"So is yours." So I reach up and have her left breast in my hand. I feel its underneath fullness inside the bra behind the cotton blouse. Her nipple is still firm and pointed as though she is always excited. Yes, my Jennifers' breasts are very beautiful.

"Get up so we can talk."

"What time is it?"

"A little after twelve."

"I haven't been asleep an hour, Jennifer. And I'm clamming tomorrow." Protest getting into my voice again.

"You can sleep when I'm not down."

"Then lie down here beside me." An excitement of my own quickly replacing the protest.

"Not tonight. We need to talk."

"It won't take long." My fingers still feeling her firm nipple inside her bra.

"You always take half the night." A naughty smile getting into her eyes.

"There isn't anything wrong with that."

"No, that part is great. But not tonight."

"When? Soon? Real soon?"

"Maybe, silly, we'll see. But get up so we can talk. I'll fix myself a scotch. Do you want scotch or a beer?" Then she is up and going toward the hall.

"Beer." And I am up and pulling on my jeans and going toward the bathroom.

"Have you seen The Waves yet?" She asks from the kitchen. "Robert has told me about it. But this evening was the first time I've seen it."

"I drove past it last week." And the water in my cupped hands cool how hot my face is. "God, are you burnt," I say to myself looking at my face in the mirror. Several dry crusted patches that look angry and about to bleed are on my cheeks. Two red splits are deep in my bottom lip. I need to stay out of the sun and wind for awhile so my skin can heal. But I can't. Or more correctly, I can but I won't.

"The grand opening is next month." Her huskiness coming softly from the kitchen. "The architect did an office building that Robert was involved in last year. His buildings are always so interesting, so conceptual. We had him over for a party last winter. He is really making a name for himself. Robert likes working with him." But I had brought her perfume into the bathroom. And tomorrow afternoon when I come in from clamming it will still be throughout the apartment as a constant reminder of Jennifer, Jennifer.

But we hate The Waves. Just as we hate all of the sudden development out on Emerald Isle. It had been a lonely pristine barrier island, and that wasn't very many years ago. Then they came in and stripped away the ancient gnarled forests down to bare sand behind the dune line. Then they started up and out with their steel and concrete and glass. They see them as good investments. We see them as horrible wounds. But we are as destructive on the water as they are destructive on the land. But we still secretly hope that a hurricane will come and clean off the mess that they have made. But they would just come back and rebuild bigger than before. So even a hurricane wouldn't change anything. But it would fill Bogue Sound behind Emerald Isle with their refrigerators and toilets and shingles. Then it would be worse than it is now with the street and yard and parking lot run off coming into it after every rain. And worse than it is now with us pounding on it day and night with our clamming and scalloping and shrimping and floundering and gillnetting. Poor Bogue Sound is being used to death.

Jennifer sits sipping scotch, her eyes bright smiling still, in the red flowered upholstered chair. "Show me before you sit down." She laughs. So I push down my jeans below my hips so she can see where the tan stops. "Isn't that hilarious! You're half white and half black. You are a picture, Keith, you really are." In summer I clam without a shirt, with only jeans and fishing boots, so I quickly become half and half and look like something you would see in a carnival.

"And you are in such great shape. God you are hard as a rock." She says in bright smiling appraisal. So I want to pose handsomely and to flex mightily and to lift something very heavy over my head if necessary to continue her praise. But instead I just smile through a blush and sit in the plaid upholstered chair. Then I reach for the beer on the end table that is between us.

"God, Keith, you are gorgeous. You really are." And her

eyes widen and her eyes flatten. And I know what that means. But I just continue to grin happily and stupidly at my Jennifer.

She always sits in that chair, and I always sit in this chair, during the many long talks that we have had these past several years. These long talks late late into the night, she in her chair, me in my chair, are a large part of whatever it is that we are together. And for days after she is gone, I cannot sit in her chair. And I try hard to not even look at her chair there empty.

"So tell me how clamming has been." Her eyes looking at me over the scotch she sips.

"Just more of the same old thing. They're still getting harder to find. Some days are really bust ass to make even decent money. And we're into the dog days again, and they get rough to take out there everyday."

"How do you do it everyday, Keith? No, why do you do it?"

"Because that's what I do."

"But why?"

"Because I'm a clammer, so I clam."

"But why?"

"Because I love it."

"But why?"

"What's this why, why, Jennifer?!" Me suddenly getting defensive with her pursuit.

"Just wondering, that's all." Her bright eyes smiling coyly over the glass as she again sips scotch.

But a fella has to be careful when talking with Jennifer. She will ask one innocently leading question one after the other until the fella gets carried away with himself and goes into brag and bluster, then she will nail him to the wall with a fast one liner like, "Well, that really doesn't seem necessary anymore," or "Are you really certain that your information is correct?". Then she casually changes the subject with a flip of her hair. But the fella is left still nailed to the wall for all to see. I know, I have learned this technique of hers the hard way.

"We're planning to go clam Ocracoke next week." Trying to get the conversation back on safer ground.

"Oh, that will be a nice trip, Keith. And you do need to get away. Maybe you can relax some and enjoy the beach. We were out there in the spring staying with friends. It was so much fun."

"But we're going to work, not to play, Jennifer."

And that brings sure enough suddenly raised eyebrows. "Oh? And all we do is play?"

And having just avoided a small nailing by getting defensive rather than bragging, now I have set myself up for a big nailing by getting into their business. But I have wanted to say this for a long time, so I say it, "Well, all the hell y'all do is run around visiting here and visiting there. That doesn't sound like very hard work to me."

Her eyebrows fall and her eyes narrow and flash. "Well, Mister High and Mighty, Robert's work is mentally difficult rather than physical difficult, if that is what you mean. And I have responsible positions in a number of organizations. You certainly do not know everything, Keith." And in her mind she stamps her foot and says, 'so there!' But I struck a nerve. But if I say anything now, it will be the wrong thing and she will nail me. So I keep my mouth shut. Seems like today is my day for doing a lot of that. So I continue to look at her without speaking. And she continues to look at me expectantly.

But it does seem as though all they do is run around visiting. Because Jennifer is always saying that she just went to Atlanta for so and so, or Robert just went to Kansas City for so and so, or they just went to Maine for so and so. The places change and the so and so's change, but their constantly running around visiting does not change. And compared to my endless bust ass routine, that doesn't sound like very hard work.

But that is their business, and therefore not my business. Because there is an invisible line which separates what we can talk about and what we cannot talk about. In general, anything here in my world is open for discussion, whether fishing or fisheries or pollution or conservation or books or movies or local politic or coastal development. But anything in her world beyond here is not open for discussion. But whenever we are together she continues to list their comings and goings. But apparently this for my information, but not for my comment. And I am usually very careful to stay out of their business. Because my Jennifer is here finally, and I do not want to make her mad so she will leave.

So for these minutes we sit staring hard at each other. Her narrowed eyes daring me to get into their business again. Me knowing damn well not to. Then her eyes begin to open and to brighten. Then she smiles prettily and holds out her glass for me to go mix another scotch, and I know that she is not leaving yet.

And from the kitchen, I can hear Jennifer moving around looking at things in the living room. There are the wood shore birds that Pete The Clammer carves so well. The ballast rock from an old sailing vessel. The copies of National Fisherman and Coastwatch and Oceans. The barnacled hand blown wine bottle. The several unique shells. The several unique pieces of driftwood, and other things. The usual things that fishermen collect and have laying around. And I can hear Jennifer moving around handling them. And it seems so good to have her here to dispel the everywhere aloneness of just me through all the days and nights. But how different we are, and how impossible it is for us to ever always be together. I own my seven year old car, my skiff, outboard and trailer, my fishing gear, the odds and ends furniture in this rented apartment, and several hundred dollars in the bank. That's it, that's me. But Jennifer's Dad had bought Burlington Industries and Cone Mills stock way back in the early days of those companies. Now she is worth several million dollars on her own. But she rarely mentions it, and she never flaunts it, but somehow you are always aware that she has it. And she is a night person and I am a day person. And she dabbles at many things while I concentrate on a few things. And she is more intelligent and better read and well traveled. And she seems quite comfortable in an arrangement marriage. But tonight Jennifer is here with me.

Now she is standing at the wide living room window that

looks down the long grassy hill to the sprawling Casper's Marina gravel yard and to its docks where shiney yachts and powerboats and sailboats are tied. And in the night beyond are the Inland Waterway channel markers, and in the distance a well lighted tug approaches pushing a darkened barge.

"I always love your view." And her huskiness is still so soft in her voice. So I put my arm around her waist and she puts her arm around my waist, and standing close beside each other we watch the tug and barge slowly approach.

So this is my world. This huge world that has long existed between the back there highlands and the far over yonder ocean. This thick soup nursery to almost every thing that is in the ocean world. This world here of low dunes and wooded marsh islands and myriad creeks that wind endlessly and mudflats and grassy marsh islands and spreading bays that open into yawning sounds And all of the thick soup smells that now come with the seabreeze to move and to billow the curtain here in this warm late night. So we turn and we kiss a slow kiss until our breathing is jagged.

"Whoa, Keith!" She says pulling back. "I forgot how well you kiss. Whew, but not right now. I have something so exciting to tell you. Let's sit down." Then she is in her flowered chair, and I am in my plaid chair, here in my world.

"Guess what?" Her bright eyes smiling.

"What?"

"Robert and I talked about it on the way down this afternoon. We are going to open a seafood market. Isn't it exciting? What do

33

you think?"

"A seafood market? Okay, I guess." Me taken completely by surprise. "But y'all don't know anything about seafood markets."

"But that's the best part. We don't need to. Because we want you to run it." As she beams with excitement.

"Me? I don't know anything about running a seafood market."

"But you know everything about seafood. And a market is just a store that sells seafood."

"I know how to catch a few kinds of seafood, but I certainly don't know everything about seafood. "

"Of course you do, silly. You would be perfect."

"Jennifer, I don't want to run a seafood market."

"Of course you do. Think of the opportunity. Think of the money we'll make. We'll be so successful." Her excitement still beaming. "The tackle shop at the Flying Bridge Marina is for lease. We're going to lease it. We'll have to knock out the back wall and build some coolers. Oh, it will need a lot of remodeling. But we'll be so successful, Keith."

But the last thing in the world I want is a land job running a seafood market. There is absolutely no way in hell that I am going to stop clamming to be a clerk in a seafood market. So I start to tell her so, when she says, "and I'll come down every weekend, and we'll run the market together."

So that stops me. Jennifer down every weekend. Jennifer and I together every weekend. That stops me. Suddenly I am silent. But my mind is going a thousand miles an hour. Because, yes, this would be perfect. Yes, this would be so much more than I now had come to think was possible. Because for the past several years, for as long as we have known each other, she would suddenly appear here in my world for a day, for several days, once for even a week, and my happiness was without bounds. But then she would just as suddenly disappear from my world, and the void and the loss was crushing. She did not write and she did not phone, for a month, for several months, once even for six months., And for however long, I was always frantic and I was always miserable. And I could not contact her in her world because she is married. And because that is her business. But she always appears again, if finally, just like tonight. And always it is as though she has never been away, just like tonight. But to soon have her here every weekend. Just the thought makes me dizzy.

But Jennifer does not like boats or fishing or the water. She does not swim and she avoids the sun and she says the wind messes her hair. But I have always felt that this is because she has always only visited here and she has never really stayed here. And if she stayed here for a length of time with someone who truly loves all these, with me, then she would come to love the water and here as much as I do. So in my mind I can see us running the market together, as we lay a bed of sparkling ice in the long display case before we carefully spread out the beautiful variety of our seafood upon it. I can see us passing over the low strong bridge to get to the docks at Harkers Island. I can see us driving down the broken shell roads to get to the docks at Sneads Ferry. I can see us carefully selecting the beautiful seafood that we will later carefully display in our market.

Then she says, "and you wouldn't have to stop clamming all together. You could clam in the mornings, then come to the market in the afternoon. But we should call it a Shoppe. Yes, that sounds much better. But what should we name it? Something with class. How about, 'Carolina Seafood Shoppe'? Yes? Maybe? No. How about, 'Gormet Seafood Shoppe'? What do you think? Or just, 'Gourmet Seafood'? I don't know. Well, we'll think about it." And her eyes have never been so bright shining. And the soft huskiness in her voice has never been so devastating.

Then in the faint grey light that is just before dawn, I stand in the street in front of my apartment, and watch Jennifer walk to her house in the next block. At the cross street she turns and waves, then in several minutes she starts up the front steps to her house. So I stand here thinking that if my wife came home at dawn half sloshed, with her makeup a mess, with her clothes wrinkled and disarrayed, it would most definitely be ass kicking time. I mean big time ass kicking with plenty to spare. I mean hollering that quickly goes to bellowing that wakes the dead. But this tonight will never be mentioned. Robert will never mention it. So I stand here wondering what manner of men these packaged men are.

But I cannot get even an hour or two of sleep. The sun is up and the birds are singing and the neighbors are moving about. But mainly it is because Jennifer's perfume is still so strong here in my bed that it seems that Jennifer is still here in my bed. So I get up and dress. And after breakfast I gather my clamming gear. Then I walk down the long grassy hill that goes to Casper's Marina where my skiff is tied. But wherever I go Jennifer's perfume goes with me.

CHAPTER FOUR

So Carl says, "What do you think?" from the next stool.

And I say, "they still act thirty going on sixteen."

And Carl says, "yeah," laughing.

"It's not funny, Carl."

And Carl say, "no," still laughing.

So I look past Wormshoe and the end of the bar to where Charlie and Jack are shooting pool, but now are arguing loudly about who has stripes and who has solids. Before this they argued about whether Jack had made a fair break. They will be arguing about God knows what next. So I say, "putting up with them for four days will get old in a hurry."

"Maybe they'll settle down once we get out there and start clamming," Carl says, but not like he believes it.

"I had hoped that we could think of a couple of other fellas."

"Me too, but we've thought of everyone. So it's them, or you and I go alone."

"But for that far out, for that long, it's best to have back ups."

So Carl nods his head, yes, in agreement with my saying what we both already know.

The four of us had just made the basic plan for Ocracoke on the dawn ferry Monday. My skiff, outboard and trailer and Carl's truck pulling them. Charlie's skiff, outboard and trailer and Jack's truck pulling them. We pool food and drinks, cooking gear, tents and camping gear so none of us will have to make a big expenditure. But then Charlie and Jack start arguing about whether Charlie's tent has dry rot, and this goes on yes, no, yes, no back and forth for five minutes. Then they start in about whether to have steak or pork chops for supper the first night. And this gets really hot and to the bar pounding stage. And in the middle of this, Larry, who is sitting several stools down, starts in about how they use to fix clam chowder in Long Island and how it is inexpensive and nutritious and filling. But the arguments that Charlie and Jack have are strictly private matters and are not for community participation, so they ignore Larry like he doesn't exist and hasn't said anything. This while Carl and I sit looking at each other in hopeless bewilderment and frustration. This while Wormshoe stands down the bar and looks at all of us like we are a bunch of God damn fools.

But everything gets settled finally.   Then Charlie and Jack go to shoot pool. And Wormshoe shakes his head sadly and walks further down the bar like he wants to get as far away from us as possible. But Larry still sits several stools down pouting and with his feelings badly hurt by being so ignored. But Carl and I do not care, not at all. Because Larry's hurt feelings are the least of our problems.

"Carl, Charlie was pretty evasive when I asked him what kind of shape his skiff and outboard are in."

"Well, he did say he hauled them last week and worked on

them."

"But he didn't say he fixed them and they're in good shape. He just said he worked on them."

"Well, they'll be in his skiff. So it's their asses."

"But if anything happens to my skiff or outboard, we'll be in his skiff too."

"Come on, Keith, don't start with the doomsday stuff. Besides, your skiff and outboard are in perfect shape."

So I nod my agreement to this. But I still would rather get whipped with a stick, than go to Ocracoke for four days with Charlie and Jack. But by now I am really tired after being up all last night with Jennifer and clamming all of today. and the thought of a cold shower and a big supper and getting to sleep early sounds really good and just what the doctor ordered. So I finish my beer in a couple of swallows. Then I stand beside my stool and toss a dollar out for Wormshoe and start collecting my loose change on the bar.

"So we'll clam tomorrow. Then Sunday we'll haul my skiff and get packed." I say belching air.

"Yeah. But we might should all meet here tomorrow afternoon to be sure everything still looks good. And we better start checking next week's weather forecast."

"Okay." But out of the corner of my eye I see Larry badly wanting to say something and starting to. So I turn to him before he can and say, "gotta go, Larry, see you tomorrow," and start for the door. But then Carl looks and sees that my going will leave him alone with Larry. So he says, "Wait, Keith, I'm going too," as he starts gulping at his beer.

But at the door I hear Jack accuse Charlie of moving his ball to a better position while Jack was gone taking a leak. Charlie pounds his cue stick butt on the floor denying it. Jack turns and hollers to Wormshoe for confirmation and support. But Wormshoe just looks at them as if to say, "I've put up with as much of y'all's shit as I'm going to." So I walk out the door shaking my head.

But when I get to my apartment, there is a note on the door from Jennifer. It says that she doesn't know how I could clam today after last night. That I am one tough man and she is proud of me. That they are having friends over tonight for drinks and a buffet starting around sevenish and for me to be sure and come because Robert wants to talk to me. And she had underlined the, Robert wants to talk to you, part several times. So right away I think, 'All right! Here we go! Robert and I are finally going to settle this about Jennifer.' But as a practical matter, an inland man, of however good shape and condition, would be wise to think twice before getting in the face of a fisherman whose everyday work defines work itself as well as it defines stamina. So right away I forget about how really tired I am. Because even though Robert has thirty pounds on me, I know I can take him easily. And Jennifer's perfume is still through out my apartment as though she were here.

But as I climb the steps that lead to their porch, my hands at my side ready to clinch into fists, Robert excuses himself from the small group of people he is talking with and comes toward me with a big smile and a hand outstretched ready to shake.

"Keith, good to see you again. Good that you could come this evening. Jennifer said you were really tan, but by god you're black. We spend fortunes to get tans half that good." And he is still shaking my hand like we are long lost buddies. "So, Jennifer said you like our seafood market idea."

But I had completely forgotten about the seafood market. And the seafood market is the last thing on my mind. So I try to think fast. "Well, it would be a money maker, Robert, that's for sure. But I don't think I'm the right man to run it." And I release my grip from the shake so he will take back his hand.

"Nonsense, Keith, you're the perfect man for it. You're a fisherman,that will be part of the draw. It will be a, 'if a fisherman recommends it, it's bound to be good,' sort of a thing. These people will flock to it. They like that sort of thing." And he waves a hand toward the chatting, well dressed friends of theirs who are standing and milling among themselves in small groups here on the porch as well as inside in the living room. But I don't think that these well dressed people will think very much of a fisherman's recommendation. But Robert sure seems to think so. "So I was telling Jennifer this afternoon that I thought we should name it, 'Capt. Keith's Seafood Shoppe.' But she didn't like it. She said it didn't have class. But I like it. What do you think?"

"Well, I don't know, Robert. That would take some getting use to." And it is all I can do to keep a straight face. But I can see that Robert is serious about liking it. But I know what the fellas at Sammy's would think about it. And I know how quickly, 'Capt.

Keith's Seafood Shoppe,' would get me laughed off the water.

"Well, think about it. Okay?" And I nod, yes. "Now, one more thing, then I'll get you a drink and introduce you around." And he leans close and says low, "don't worry about the financial part. You'll be well taken care of. Okay?" And I nod, yes, again. "Okay." He says settling it. And as we turn to walk inside I am afraid that he is about to put his arm around my shoulder like we are long lost buddies.

But the rage has to still be there. The rage simply has to still be there, even if it is buried somewhere deep inside where he forced it to go so he wouldn't have to deal with it. Because that much rage simply cannot be shrugged off and forgotten about completely, even by so packaged a controlled man. Because early one morning, soon after Jennifer and I met and soon after our late all night things started, I was down on my skiff at Casper's Marina doing maintenance before going out to clam. Except for the gulls bitching and whirling and squabbling among themselves high overhead which they always do, it was quiet and calm and the yachts and the powerboats were motionless in their slips with their tie lines slack. I had a spark plug out and was checking it for wear when I saw a movement among the boats out where the dock teed in the deeper water. My eyes looked up without raising my head, and I saw that it was Robert. He looked as though he had been suddenly aroused from sleep without washing his face or combing his hair, then had gone through a loud argument with shouting and accusations, but when nothing was resolved he had brought all of his unspent rage here to direct it at me from a distance. But he just walked back and forth, back and forth, arms stiff and shoulders hunched and face twisted, hidden behind the tied boats without ever taking his eyes off me and without ever approaching me. So I took my time and did more maintenance than I had intended to do, so he could let the rage build until it boiled and there was a face to face confrontation. But when I looked again he was gone. He simply swallowed his rage at me and walked away. Now we are long lost buddies thinking about going into a business together. So, yes, it is difficult for me to really take Robert seriously.

Their wide living room and side kitchen are separated by a long mahogany bar for eating at or drinking at or just gathering at. Jennifer looks truly delicious in a soft yellow print summer dress that is off her so white shoulders as she busys herself with spreading the buffet plates and bowls along the bar. When Robert and I walk in the front door, she bright smiles me as only she can with her black black hair shimmering still, so I fall in love with her all over again. She certainly stands out in a crowd. She certainly attracts attention. She can walk into a room full of strangers and in fifteen minutes most of them are standing around her and hanging onto her every word and waiting impatiently for their turn to speak with her personally. It is amazing how she can massage a crowd without ever seeming to do so. It is amazing how strangers immediately become her friends without ever realizing their sudden transformation. And long after meeting her once, you can hear them say, 'Oh yes, I know Jennifer Ryan quite well, we are good friends.' It is really amazing how she can have that effect on people.

So Robert takes me to each chatting group and introduces me as, 'Keith Englund, Jennifer's fisherman friend.' But I don't like how innocent that sounds. But I don't know what else I am either. And they look at me like I am a trophy that he has just brought from safari. So right away I feel uncomfortable by how different I am from them. So I try to small talk like they small talk. But I don't know how to small talk like they small talk. So I just smile and say hello, smile and say hello. So now I feel stupid and bumbling also. And my face seems frozen in a big grin like a possum chewing nails. But there doesn't seem to be an end to the chatting groups that Robert takes me to meet. And Robert seems to be enjoying all this too much. And I just want to escape, and my heart is pounding, and the no sleep last night and the all day clamming brings a serge of weariness. So the endless faces and voices blur. Then Robert is smiling at me and saying for me to mingle, that these are important people for me to know for the seafood market. Then he excuses himself and goes to talk intently with a tall balding very distinguished looking man whose name I cannot remember. The muscles in my face twitch from the long forced big grin. Then I find a corner to stand in. Then Jennifer brings me a plate of mostly sliced turkey and sliced ham and I realize that I am half starved. So she stands close and we talk low just for each other and I begin to feel better. But then she says that she has to get back to the buffet table, and for me to mingle, and she will see me in a little while. So

I back myself further into the corner and wolf at the food.

"So you're the, 'Keith Englund, Jennifer's fisherman friend,' that I've heard so much about." And her hair is more red than blonde, and her face and arms are thoroughly freckled, and she is almost cute. "I'm Billie Griffin, Jennifer's old college roommate from Charlotte." And she shakes my hand firmly and strongly. "Just arrived. The traffic was murder all the way. I hate driving. So, let's see what we have here." Then she leans back and looks me up and down in appraisal. "Well, no raving hunk, but I guess you'll do in a lean and hungry sort of way." And smiling, she becomes cute and almost pretty. "Jennifer sent me over for moral support before you back yourself through the wall trying to get away from these people." Then she laughs easily and smoothly, so I laugh too. "Can't say that I blame you. Most of these people have more money than god. And that makes the rest of us nervous. But I'm just a poor old eight grade school teacher. Jennifer invites me for weekends now and then so I can see how the other half lives. And a peek now and then is enough. Then I hurry home to Charlotte even more happy with my low salary and long hours and stack of mortgages. And my eleven year old son who eats me out of house and home. And my ex who is always late with his child support checks. This lady has the good life and I know it. So what about you?"

"I'm single, never married."

"I know that, silly, Jennifer tells me everything. Well, not everything, but enough. I mean what about you and these people?"

"I dig clams for a living. That says it all."

"But do these people make you nervous? Well, obviously they do the way you've backed yourself in this corner. Do they make you envious? Do you have the 'I wishes'?

"No."

"Sure?"

"I'm sure."

"Good. Didn't think you would. Well, I hoped you wouldn't. I don't either. Never have. When you get to know them, they aren't really nice people. But we're nice people, aren't we?" And her cute smiling is catching. And her abruptness is fun once you get use to it. "So, Mr. Famous Fisherman, tell me about clams and clamming."

"What do you want to know?" I say laughing now.

"Everything. Tell me everything. I'm all ears."

"That would take hours, days even."

"I'm here until Sunday afternoon."

"Well, I can quickly tell you more than you ever really wanted to know about clams, Billie. And I don't want to bore you."

"No, I'm serious, Keith, I really want to know. We're getting into the estuaries and the ocean in my science class. And any first hand knowledge will help me to teach my kids."

"Then you should go clamming with me. When you see it while I explain it, you will understand it better."

"Great! When?"

"Well, I'm going tomorrow."

"Great! What time, what should I wear, what do I do?"

So I say that any old knock around clothes will be fine. And she says that Robert probably has some, but for me not to expect her to look like a fashion plate in them. So I laugh and say that if the clams don't mind, I won't. And she laughs. So I tell her that I tool clam with either a bullrake or a pearake, but that she can hand clam in the shallows near me because hand clamming is a lot easier. So she asks what a bullrake and a pearake are. And I try to describe and explain them but it quickly gets confusing to her, so I just say that I will show her tomorrow. Then I say that I stay out for six or seven hours and that that might be too long a hot day for her since she isn't use to it. So she says that if she wilts I can just drag her over and dump her in the bottom of my skiff until I finish work. And we both laugh.

Then Jennifer comes over to us standing in the corner, the buffet over and the chatting still people milling and mingling and seriously into drinking now. But when Billie tells her that she is going clamming with me in the morning, all Jennifer says is, "Won't that be nice." And there is a flatness in her voice. But by now, my long weariness really begins to sweep over me until I feel light headed. So I tell them that I am going home, that it has been a long day and that I am beat. And I tell Billie to be at my skiff down at Casper's at eight, but that if she changes her mind about going that will be okay. But she just says simply, "I'll be there, Keith." But when I look at Jennifer, she is looking at me hard and with a flatness in her eyes also. But I am just too tired to wonder about that now, so I just say my good nights to them. Then I find Robert in the crowd and say goodnight. And he says for me to come over tomorrow evening so we can really talk about the seafood market. So I say that I will, but I already know that I won't.

CHAPTER FIVE

"Good morning, Keith." She says brightly as she comes along the dock towards me stowing gear in my skiff.

"Good morning, Billie." And our voices echo quickly among the nearby boats and then go out across the calm water.

She stops here at the end of the dock above my skiff and puts her arms up and out and says, "da dah!" and does a circle. "Aren't I absolutely ravishing?" And I have to laugh at how rag dolly she looks. She is wearing beat up sneakers and a pair of Robert's knock around Khaki pants with all the extra material gathered at her waist by a belt and the leg bottoms rolled up several times to reduce length and a baggy teeshirt. Her more red than blonde hair is pulled into two side pony tails with rubber bands holding them, and here in the direct sun all of her many freckles are very prominent.

"Stunning, ma'am. Simply stunning."

"You are laughing with me, and not at me. Aren't you?"

"Oh, with you. Yes, with you."

"And damn well you better be, if you know what's good for you", Still brightly happy.

"Oh, I forgot to tell you not to wear a bra and panties. The silt you stir up will get into them and they will never come clean."

"How dare you, sir! Right away telling a lady to take off her bra and panties, and we hardly know each other." And she has that wonderful excitement that all inlanders have when they are about to go for a boatride. "If you must know, I'm not wearing a bra. But I'm not about to take off my panties now."

"Okay." And now I have the excitement also. Because it will be a fun day having Billie with me. So I put up my hand for her to take as she steps down into the skiff. Then she is standing on the bottom with her hands out as the skiff rocks some.

"We aren't tipping over, are we?"

"No. You're quite safe. She's a seventeen foot by six foot flat bottom skiff. Very seaworthy. And she'll carry a big load. She's bad about throwing spray in rough water, but hopefully we won't have any of that. You'll sit here on the bow seat and I'll sit there in the stern steering. There are life preservers under the bow seat if you want to wear one."

"Do I need to?"

"Not really, but it may make you feel safer."

"I feel safe right now. I'll see how I feel after we get going."

"Okay. I brought you a double decker peanut butter and jelly sandwich and a brownie and a jug of water for lunch. They're in the stern seat there."

"Rather plain fare isn't it, sir, or is it Captain?"

"I 'm the Captain, but you can call me Keith." Me smiling at this already being fun.

"Captain Keith, sir!" She says saluting. And her eyes are wide with excitement now.

"And plain fare for a reason. Anything with mayonnaise spoils quickly. Peanut butter and jelly are filling and nutritious and not heavy. Heavy foods in this heat will make you sick. And water because soft drinks don't really quench your thirst. Drink plenty of water so you don't get dehydrated."

"You've given this lots of thought."

"Mainly just learned the hard way. Ready?"

"Ready, Captain Keith."

So I crank the outboard and while it idles I loose the sternline, then I step around Billie sitting on the bow seat and loose the bowline and push the bow out and away from the dock, then I step around her again and go and sit on the stern seat. Then I give the outboard a little gas to gain steerage in the tide, and we begin to pull away from Caspers' slowly.

"Don't stand while we're underway, okay? You don't have sealegs yet."

"Okay."

"You should sit facing forward, Billie, not facing me, okay? Facing aft tends to make people seasick when they aren't use to the water."

"Okay."

But I am telling her too much too soon, because I can see some apprehension in her eyes now that we are underway so I shut up. Now we are away from Caspers' and into the Inland Waterway and I keep increasing the gas gradually until we are planed off and running along smoothly. But we only run up the Waterway about a mile before I start to back off the gas and get ready to dock at the dock behind Walt's where he sells clam licenses and has a convenience store and an outboard repair shop combined. I introduce Walt to Billie and tell him she's never clammed and I'm taking her out to show her how. So right away he turns to her and says, "well, you'll be learning from one of the best, Miss Griffin." So Billie looks at me and smiles proudly. And I stand here grinning and feeling real good about myself. So while Walt writes out her license, I go get us a coke and cheese nabs and come back and tell Billie that these will calm her stomach and she thanks me and she means it. Then I tell Walt how it seems like my gear shifting lever is losing some of its crispness when I shift gears. And he nods knowingly and says that it's my shifting mechanism inside. That they're made of plastic so they begin to wear quickly and that's why I'm loosing crispness. So he goes and gets a replacement kit, and I pay him for everything. Then the three of us stand and small talk about this and that for a few minutes while Billie and I finish our cokes and nabs. Then I remember rubber gloves to protect her fingers against shell cuts while she's hand clamming. So Walt goes and gets a pair. Then Billie and I start for my skiff.

Now we are planed off and running the Waterway smoothly again. And I can feel the getting higher sun begin to tingle my already burnt skin. On our right are small marsh islands and mudflats with small shallow creeks separating them. Then behind these are larger wooded islands, and I can see white herons roosting on branches of some of the trees. So I point them out to Billie and she nods excitedly. Then there in the distance are the high backside dunes of Bear Island. On our left are several miles of side by side waterfront homes and cottages with their docks and tied boats. Most are occupied and have swimsuits and towels drying on their clotheslines and beachballs and rafts around their lawns. But some are vacant, and these look forlorn. Then we close with an expensive yacht going south, so I back off the gas so my skiff will take its thick rolling wake gently. Then we are planed off again, and now on our right is the long blue green channel that goes straight to Bogue Inlet with the ocean a hazy white beyond it. Now bigger creeks and bigger marsh islands on both sides, with several piled up shell banks from Waterway dredging here and there. Then the real high bridge that goes across overhead to Emerald Isle with the cars on it looking small and bright in the morning sun. Now the lesser bays begin now that Bogue Sound itself has begun. I had decided that we would clam Bogue Sound because the run to it is long enough to be enjoyable, but not so long that it is tiring. And because the run passes the best variety of estuary life and scenery. And because the run passes plenty of places to run to in case of breakdown or storm. But what clouds there are, are thin and stringy, and the light warm wind is southwest which is good. But by noon it will be ninety, ninety-five and stifling and the hard glare will start. But hopefully the thunderstorm will not come later in the afternoon to spoil all this for Billie.

Now she is laid out on her stomach in the water feeling for

clams like I showed her in the sandy grassy shallows a little way from the bank. I am waist deep out in the Sound bullraking the packed shelly bottom there. Then I catch a seahorse in the bullrake basket. So I bring it cupped in both hands to where Billie is. And right away she starts to ouu and ahh at the beautiful sea animal. But when she sits up to take the seahorse in her cupped hands, her teeshirt clings to her chest and I see her freckled small breasts and their pointed red nipples. So she sees the cling and she pulls her teeshirt loose. Then she looks up at me and smiles and shrugs, 'oh well.'

"There's a long sleeve flannel shirt in the skiff that you can put on. You might should put it on now anyway before you burn. And there's probably a floppy hat of some kind in there too. This sun gets to you fast when you're not use to it."

"You're a nice man, Keith. And a gentleman. And you think of everything." And she looks up at me with appreciation. And now she has the seahorse cupped in her hands and the ouus and the ahhs begin again. "Oh, he is so beautiful. I am actually holding a real seahorse, Keith, oh." But the animal is terrified and it bends and twists and stretches as best it can to get away. "Oh, poor thing, oh you poor beautiful thing." So she puts it in the water in her cupped hands until it is deep enough to swim free. Then it disappears quickly among the eelgrass as it heads for the deeper water. "Oh Keith, this is the most wonderful thing that has ever happened to me. I have actually held a wild sea animal in my hands. Thank you. Oh."

So I start to get choked up by the wonder too, but I just say, "well, I better get back to work."

Now we are sitting in the skiff having lunch. "--- so the clam spawn just floats around on top of the water for a week or so until it senses other clams beneath it, then it drops and burrows and sets itself in the bottom. A clam can be male or female or both at once, whatever it senses is needed most at that time. They can move up in the bottom in summer for cool, or down in the bottom in winter for warmth, but they can't move to another place. Where they first settle is where they stay. Their best defense is staying hidden in the grass or in the dead shells. And of course having thick shells. But everything out here is after them. Crabs, whelks, fish, rays, shrimp, everything. And of course us. They spawn in the millions, but their mortality is very high. Only a few live to maturity. But with a great deal of luck a very few live for forty or fifty years. Clams are a remarkable sea animal, they really are."

But now I stop talking. Because a person can absorb just so much so quickly when they come out here. Whether it is their first time or their ten thousandth time. It is every thing, the wind, the tide, the weather, the sky, the mudflats, the islands, the grasses, the rivers, the bays, the sounds. The fishes, the animals, the birds. The all and the everything in a sudden assault on sight and smell and hearing and feeling. It all is so huge and it all is so critical and it all is so complicated and it all is so staggering. It is the most beautiful church and it is the most beautiful religion that there ever can be. So for this while we can only sit in the skiff and finish our lunch in silence.

"There just wasn't any way that I could understand until now." She says quietly.

"Understand what, Billie?" And I speak quietly also.

"What y'all do, where y'all do it. But mostly,why y'all do it."

"But we're loving it to death."

"But that too is understandable."

The thunderstorm does not come, and I am glad about that for Billie's sake. She probably would have weathered it just fine, and she may even have found it exciting. But she has already had a fairly full day of excitement, so it's not coming suits me. I endure thunderstorms, but I certainly don't like them. But
one did start to build in the west about two o'clock. I saw the greys and blues form as they quickly become much darker as they billow and pile and roll higher in that direction about that time. And several times I thought I heard deep long rumbles coming from there. But if it did build and then break finally, it stayed far inland of us.

So just before four we make the run down the Waterway back to Swansboro under puffy white clouds and plenty of left over heat and a beginning to slant hard sun. But we make the run without talking. Billie sits on the bow seat with one hand holding on the floppy hat in the wind, and her other hand shading her eyes against the glare, and the tail of the flannel shirt flapping out behind her. She swivels her neck looking left, then right, then looking left again in an effort to see everything and to take in everything so she can remember everything. And I enjoy the run because she enjoys the run so much. The clam buyer is just south of Casper's. And as we run past Casper's we can see the entire Swansboro waterfront to the right of it. And seeing a town from the water gives you a totally different perspective than from the land so that for the first time you can see the real reason for its being where it is and for its being laid out the way it is. And however many times that Billie has been to Swansboro, I can tell by how intently she is looking at its waterfront that she is now seeing it in its real perspective as that of a very old fishing village for fishermen and their families.

And when I come out of the clam buyer's building and start walking his dock to my skiff, Billie turns on the bow seat and holds a finger to her lips for me to be quiet, then she points to five dolphin that are rolling and blowing and frolicking as they pass near by going south. So I quietly watch them until they are out of sight also. Then Billie looks up at me on the dock above her, and she smiles real big and her eyes begin to glisten.

When I step in my skiff and hand her twelve dollars, she says, "what's this for?"

"Your pay. One hundred and twenty clams at ten cents each."

"No, Keith, that isn't why I went." And she tries to hand it back. "Put it toward your gas."

"No I was going anyway. You did the work, that's your pay."

So I don't plane my skiff going back to Casper's. Rather I just cruise slowly to give Billie one last look at everything. So she looks long across the small marshes and the wooded islands to the backside dunes at Bear Island. Then she looks long at how Swansboro is tiered low at the waterline then rises like carefully placed steps so that the houses four blocks in still have a view across the water, with the best view of all being from the old old houses that have widow walks. Billie looks very tired and very happy as she holds her twelve dollars in both hands and looks. So I think to myself, 'how quickly she could become one of us.'

CHAPTER SIX

Carl had already come and gone by the time I get to Sammy's. But Wormshoe says that he said to tell me that everything is still go for him for Ocracoke, and that he will stop by my apartment in the morning and help me haul my skiff. Then Wormshoe says that we are salty sons of bitches to go clam Ocracoke for four days sleeping on a marsh island. That he and Sammy trawled the Pamlico Sound plenty of times before Sammy lost his trawler, but that the Pamlico Sound always made them real nervous somehow. That the Atlantic Ocean is more friendly, more predictable. Because the Pamlico Sound is nothing but a widow maker, and that it is a whole hell of a lot of unruly water for us to be stuck out in the middle of. So I say, "yeah Wormshoe, but you're a candy ass and we're hard asses." That the tougher and the scarier things get, the better we like them. That we're clamming fools for sure. And that if it was easy clamming there, these other candy asses here would go do it. But since it isn't, us hard asses will go show all you candy asses how it's done. So Wormshoe opens and closes his mouth several times, then sputters and stutters for awhile before he can finally say, "yeah, yeah, yeah, think you're smart don't you, real smart? Well let the Pamlico Sound pucker your asshole one time, just one time, and one of these trips it will, then come back here and tell me how hard an ass you are, if you're still living to do it." Then he stomps down the bar shaking his head and talking to himself, because Wormshoe is pissed at me.

So I sit grinning at myself in the mirror that is behind the bar, because I enjoy ragging Wormshoe now and then to see how his mouth starts working open, close, open, close as the sputtering and stuttering starts. Then I look down the bar now that my eyes have adjusted, and see that Larry is busy at the slot machine that is set up with poker hands. And I remember how tight it is set, and how much money I have lost in it, and how I have promised myself that I will never play it again. Then I see Jack shooting pool by himself, so I start for that end of the bar. I say hello as I pass Larry, and he says that he had won fifteen dollars but that it is taking it back fast now so it won't be much longer. So I say okay. Then Jack and I say hello. And Jack says that Charlie just left, but that everything is still go for them for Ocracoke. And I say, good. Then I ask him what kind of shape Charlie's outboard and skiff are in. And he says, "ragged as hell as usual." And that Charlie likes things ragged. That if something isn't ragged when he gets it, he soon gets it ragged enough to suit him. But that they clammed with them today and that they did all right, so they should make the trip all right. So I tell him that the trip could quickly become a ballbuster with ragged gear, because the Pamlico Sound simply does not give a damn. But he just says, "well you can't tell that dumb son of a bitch anything." Then Wormshoe brings the beer I just motioned for, and I say, "sorry about that back there, Wormshoe, just kidding." Because I don't want him pissed at me for very long. And he says, "you'll see I'm right, smart ass. One of these trips, you'll see." But he is smiling, so I know that everything is okay between us.

So I turn back to Jack and say that I hope he and Charlie can get along out there. Because once we are out there we are stuck with each other for four days, day and night. So he says for me just to tell Charlie to quit messing with his wife. So I say that I thought that you were divorced. So he says, "we are, but I still don't want him humping her every night." And the logic in that escapes me. But I keep going and say that I hear that he is messing with Charlie's girlfriend, so that should make the swap about even. But he just says, "I am. Serves the son of a bitch right. But he better quit humping my wife, if he knows what's good for him." Then he goes back to playing himself pool. So I go back and sit on a stool midway down the bar so I won't have to talk to Jack anymore. And I sit here and hate like hell that Carl and I have to have, or at least should have, back-up fellas and a back-up outboard and skiff, going also. Then Larry sits on the stool beside me.

"It took the fifteen I won, plus ten more of my money."

"Yeah, it took me for twenty last week. But I'm through with it."

"Yeah, me too." But neither of us are and we know it. Then Larry starts to slow turn his beer in it's wet circles like he does. And I sit here and look at my grim black face in the mirror and hope like hell that Larry isn't about to start some shit because I'm really not in the mood for it.

"So, is everything set for Ocracoke?"

"Seems to be." And I feel myself begin to cringe. "Still nothing unusual in the forecast for next week." But he does seem sober for a change.

"Well, be real careful out there, Keith. You know how fast the water can get tricky and mean."

"Yeah, and thanks." But if he was going to start some shit, right then was when he would have started it, but he doesn't. And I appreciate his concern, as well as Wormshoe's. But then fishermen always have concern for each other because we have been there and we know how the water can get.

"I'd go, but my arthritis bothers me enough around here. Sleeping on a marsh island would kill me." And he starts opening and closing his big flat hands and flexing his fingers like he is trying to loosen them up. Because the constant manual labor and the constant dampness does eventually get us in the muscles and the joints. "Thirty some years of working the water has just about ruined me. Didn't use to feel it, but the last few years I've sure started to. But working the water is all I know, all I've ever done. And all I've ever wanted to do. And it was the same with my old man. Work the water is all he ever did. All he ever wanted to do." And Larry begins a small smile as he remembers. "I never told you this. We lived on a derelict fishing scow tied to a buyer's dock in Shinnecock, New York, south of Long Island Sound. That was way before development started out there. Just a bunch of fishing villages scattered around all the bays before you get to the Sound. But a great place for a kid growing up. And that scow was the only home I knew until I got grown. That and out on the water everyday with the old man. But mom hated it, all of it. She and the old man argued about it all the time. Then we came home one night and she had moved out. Clothes, everything of hers gone. No note, nothing. So I asked the old man where mom went. And he said that he guessed she had bigger fish to fry. Only that. And we never mentioned her again. We oystered some, and bay scalloped some. But mostly we clammed. The old man was damn good with tongs, the best I've ever seen. And I got to be a good tonger too, but not nearly as good as the old man. And god, Keith, was that scow cold in the winter." And he nudges my arm on the bar and now he is really smiling as he remembers. "Jesus, I've never known such cold. Makes me shiver just thinking about it. And leak, that old scow leaked so bad we had to pump her morning and night and in between. The old hand bilge pump, you've seen pictures of them with a handle like the old water pumps we use to have. I logged many an hour as a kid manning that pump. The old man sitting at the galley table with his evening pint saying, 'faster, son, faster, she's gaining on you.' Those were good days, Keith, they really were. Don't sound like it, but they really were. My schooling was pretty much catch as catch can. Got enough reading and writing and arithmetic to get by with the buyer, and that seemed enough. When the old man died when I was twenty, the buyer paid for the burial, then I clammed all that summer to pay him back. But the old man's skiff and all his fishing gear were mine. Then I moved into a partitioned off corner of the net storage building on the dock, so the buyer could haul the old scow and burn her. She really was an eye sore, and there was no amount of pumping that could keep her afloat by then. And between working the water and helping out the buyer around the dock, it was a good life. Real good. His name was Shingledecker. Wayne Shingledecker. Funny name. But he always treated me and the old man fair. Bought whatever we caught, and paid us fair. Wonder whatever happened to him? Probably long dead now. He was up in years even back then. God, I haven't thought about all this in years." And his eyes are glistening. So I motion to Wormshoe for two beers. And I sit here really enjoying myself because fishermen never tire of hearing about the old days on the water. "I married a couple of years later, and moved the wife into that corner of the net storage building. But she didn't like any of it, never did, and she never was satisfied. And we argued about it a lot just like mom and the old man had. Then, just like mom, one evening when I came home, she had moved out. No note, nothing, just gone. So I guessed she had bigger fish to fry, just like mom. And I never tried marriage again, and neither did the old man. Picking up a woman in a bar for the night now and then was enough after that. I signed on ocean trawlers a couple of times for the bigger paycheck, but they're too crowded and too noisy and too much like a regular job. And I always came back to working the bays alone in my skiff because that's where I belong. Even bought an old fixer-upper trawler one time that I was going to rig out one-man so I could work half way warm in the winter, when you froze to death in a skiff and had to break ice before you could clam the bays. But I was such a terrible engine mechanic I never could keep her running. And the repairs were endless and expensive, so I sold her. You can't beat a skiff and outboard for dependability and low costs, even if you do freeze to death and have to break ice before you can clam. But by then it had gotten so you could walk across Long Island Sound just on the fishing boats. Everyone was out doing it, so no one could make any money. So I just packed up and moved down to Crisfield, Maryland on the Virginia line. I oystered the Chesapeake out of there for a lot of years, and those were real good years too. Real good. But the people there are slow to warm up to strangers, if they ever do. But good people though once they get to know you, give you the shirt off their back. But by a couple of years ago the run off coming into the Chesapeake had about wiped out the oysters. So I just packed up and started driving south along the coast. When I first saw Swansboro, I thought that it would be a nice place to fish out of for awhile. And it has been. Real nice. So here I am."

Then Wormshoe brings the beers that Larry motioned for. And neither of us say anything for a few minutes. And my eyes are glistening too.

"But it's about over with here too, isn't it Keith?"

"Yeah, just about. There's a few more years yet. But scraping out a living is getting tougher and tougher."

66

"Talked with a fella a while back who said that Georgia has pretty good oystering and clamming just south of Savannah. Might try there next. And it's warmer there too. The cold really bothers my arthritis now. Then maybe down to the Florida Keys after Georgia. It's always warm there. But then I will have gone as far south as I can go. But by then I guess it won't matter much anyway."

So Larry is the last generation of father to son, father to son bay fishermen. They say that progress is great, but there can be a lot of hurt that comes with it.

"Well, guess I better go, Larry. I'm about starved."

"Yeah, me too. Look, have a good trip to Ocracoke, okay?"

"Yeah. I really like it out there, and I'm really looking forward to going."

"And, again, be careful. Hear?"

"Yeah, Larry, and thanks. And Larry, I really enjoyed this."

"Yeah, me too. Haven't thought about all that in years. See you when you get back." So we shake hands as we leave.

There are small groups of chatting people all along Jennifer's front porch. I have to slow way down to get by the cars parked on both sides of the road. I don't see Jennifer or Robert or Billie, but I wave as I go by anyway. But there's no way in hell I'm going to shower and change and come back to that mess, even if I did tell Robert I would. Last night was enough of those people. Never again. Because they don't have anything to do with me and my life. And I don't have anything to do with them and their lives.

And I know now that Jennifer won't come to see me late tonight. Because Robert's knowing is one thing. But the others can think what they want, but Jennifer won't rub their noses in it like she rubs Robert's nose in it.

CHAPTER SEVEN

I didn't set the alarm, so it is a little after eight when I awake. And the extra sleep feels good. And not having to get right up and start doing things is nice. But the muscles in my shoulders and arms and hands, my clamming muscles, are still sore and tight and I know that they need a lot more rest. But today will be slack with the getting ready to go, and tomorrow will be slack with the traveling, so they will have to settle for that much rest. But from Tuesday until Friday these same clamming muscles will have a hard row to hoe for sure. But they will hoe that row because they are good muscles and they always do what I ask of them.

So I move my head on the pillow, and right away I smell a wisp of Jennifer's perfume that still lingers from Friday night. Then right away I see her asleep in her bed in the next block. Her mouth is in a small pout and her breathing is shallow and regular. Her black black hair shines against the pillow in the morning sunlight that comes broken through the window blinds. Her hands are curled close to her face and her skin is pale white and clear. And she will sleep until noon like she usually does. But this about her being a night person and my being a day person is one of the reasons why it will not work for us. Just too much conflict in the different schedules over the long haul. But there is no 'us', not really. Never has been, never will be, so don't worry about different schedules. And the seafood market is just more of their dabbling in this, then dabbling in that. Just like their constant go go going, visiting here and visiting there, is dabbling. Anything to entertain themselves so they never get bored. Anything to occupy themselves so they never really have to face themselves. But that is their business. And therefore is not my business. But having Jennifer here every weekend, just the thought makes me dizzy. But that will never happen either.

Then I realize how hungry I am, half starved even, even though I had a big supper last night. So I lie here and wonder what to have for breakfast, what sounds good. Because anticipation is half the fun. Bacon and eggs and grits. Yes. Eggs over easy, then cut them up with the yokes all runny and piled on in with the grits until mixed up into a great tasting ugly mess. Yes. Plenty of salt and pepper and butter. Yes. Toast with strawberry jam. Yes. Plenty of hot sweet coffee. Yes to all that. Yes. Because I have learned to be good to myself whenever I can, to treat myself special whenever I can. Because I put great physical demands upon myself day in and day out for month after month. And breakfast and lunch on clamming days are usually light. So I do not scrimp on supper. If shrimp sounds good, I'll stop by the dock and buy two double hands full of fresh mediums to boil tender pink and fix fries and coleslaw, and then eat the whole damn thing. Or if a T-bone sounds good, I'll stop by the supermarket and buy the biggest one they have to fry with onion and bake a potato with butter and fix a lettuce and tomato and mayonnaise salad, and then eat the whole damn thing. Or flounder, I'll stop by the dock and buy a good long thick one to broil with lemon and fix fries and coleslaw again, and then eat the whole damn thing. Because I always clean my plate then smack my lips. Because I burn a lot of fuel doing what I do. So I don't scrimp on my fuel. And anticipation is half the fun. And I treat myself special whenever I can.

But you have to learn to keep your debt to a minimum and to live modestly when you are a fisherman. Because you lose a lot of days during the year to extended storms and winds and tides. And because your total income is small to begin with. So credit is out, or at least used only when absolutely necessary. Because you do not know what will happen tomorrow. And since you get paid in cash, your world becomes a cash world. If you want something, and you have the cash, you get it. If you want something, and you do not have the cash, you just continue wanting it until finally you have the cash. Because you do not know what will happen tomorrow. But you maintain your gear no matter what other things you have to do without. And you get rigged to work other fisheries, in spite of the small income and the lost days and the current maintenance costs. Because if there is any hope of your continuing to be a fisherman in this time of dying fisheries that hope is in your becoming versatile. In your having several sized boats and the variety of gear so that you can fish several fisheries at the height of their season when the quantities are the greatest and the prices are the strongest. But that takes sacrifice and that takes planning. Because there is only one you, and you can only do so much. And

I have known for some time that my only hope is for me to now expand into fishing for shrimp and fish in addition to my now fishing for clams and scallops. But that will take a bigger boat, and bigger boats are expensive. But Oscar Schneider has his twenty five foot trawler the 'Secret Woman' up for sale, and she is a magnificent small trawler. But to me now, ten thousand dollars is all the money in the world.

So I begin to rummage through the gear in storage on my back porch. I get the two man tent that Carl and I went in on and bought two summers ago, and spread it out on the lawn and check it for tears and dry rot. It is in good shape, so I bundle it tight again and return it to it's bag. Then I check the tent poles and they are all there, and I check the tent stakes and they are all there. Then I unroll my sleeping bag and turn it inside out and throw it across the clothesline to air. Then I get my two coolers and rinse them out with the hose and leave them open and on end to drain. Then I go back into the kitchen and begin to rummage through the cabinets and drawers for the pots and pans and utensils that I will take. And the excitement begins. Because tomorrow I return to Ocracoke and then to Shell Castle. And standing on Shell Castle looking south, Core Sound is so far in the distance that I can see the curvature of the earth.

Then Carl comes in a little before noon, and he has the excitement in his eyes also. Because going to Ocracoke is always an adventure, and commercial clammers do love adventure so. So we hook my boat trailer to his truck and take it down to

Casper's. And while Carl backs the trailer down the ramp, I go get my skiff and bring it around the dock and we load it on the trailer. Then we haul it and take it up the gravel yard out of everyone's way because Sunday is a busy boater day at Casper's and unhook it from the truck and block it up at the tongue with a cinderblock and tie down my skiff securely. Then I top off my three six gallon fuel tanks with the proper oil and gas mixture. Then Carl and I begin going through the sea compartments to make sure about the life preservers and the throw cushion and the whistle and the spare anchor and the several flashlights and the extra lengths of spare line just in case. My toolbox with its hammer and screwdrivers and wrenches and pliers and sockets, the spare spark plugs, the sheathed hunting knife, the spare coil, some string, several blocks of wood, the spare power pack, electrical tape, the spare pull cord just in case. Carl and I pulling these out and naming them to the other then putting them back where they belong. Then I take a few minutes to go ahead and install the new gear shifting assembly that I got from Walt, then I wipe off the old assembly and put it in the kit bag and put it with the other spares. While I do this, Carl checks the lower unit oil of my outboard.

While all of this is going on, two weekend boater guys in their khaki shorts and button down shirts and deckshoes uniforms stop by and ask us what we are doing and where we are going. We tell them, which opens the conversation so they can share with us their expertise on boats and boating so their girlfriends can see them talking with fishermen.

Then Carl's wife, Sara, drives up with their son, Jamie. And the excitement is in her eyes just as it is in our eyes. Because Sara is as proud of Carl's being a fisherman as Carl is proud of being a fisherman, and I envy him that. So she asks what we think of her going to the supermarket for the things to go home and fry chicken and fix potato salad for our trip over tomorrow, and right away Carl and I say that sounds great. Then she asks me how things have been, and I say a whole lot of the same old thing and she says yeah, but that things will be a little easier on us once the dog days end and the everyday heat eases and I say yeah. Then she says for me to watch out for her Carl on the trip, and I laugh and say Sara it probably will be the other way around. So she smiles proudly at Carl and says she better go on to the supermarket. So Carl kisses her and Jamie goodbye even though he probably just kissed them goodbye an hour before and he will be kissing them hello in several hours, and I envy him that also. Because a fisherman who has a fisherman's wife rather than just a wife has a huge advantage over the rest of us fishermen. So I look up the hill and see that the people have already started gathering at Jennifer's for a light lunch and some drinks and some small talk. And the contrast between her world and my world seems hopeless and like something you would read about in a silly novel. But there it is, so I feel helpless also. So Carl and I leave and go to the Riverview Restaurant and have a hamburger and a beer sitting at a table out on the wide deck that is built out over the water so it looks back down the length of Swanboro's waterfront towards Casper's. But the tourists sitting around us keep staring at us, burnt tans and sun bleached blonde hair and faded shirts and faded jeans and fishing boots, and finally it really does get uncomfortable so we hurry and finish eating.

Then we go find Charlie and Jack at Jack's house. They also have excitement in their eyes and they are getting along and they are not arguing and Carl and I welcome the hell out of that. Charlie's skiff is hauled and tied secure on his trailer, and they pretty well have their gear gathered and ready to load. But when I look at the skiff's stern, I see that it had been cut completely loose from the hull, then joined again but only with metal corner brackets and the joint just caulked. I ask Charlie if he thinks it will hold what with all the outboard motor stress there, and he says oh hell yeah no problem. He says that when he bought the skiff last month it had several bad cracks and bubbly places in the fiberglass there, so he cut the whole stern off and trimmed and sanded everything ready for refiberglassing. But then kept putting if off until he really had to get back clamming, so he fixed it this way until he had the time to fix it the right way later. But oh hell yeah the stern will hold just fine with just brackets and caulk for the trip, because he had been clamming with it this way around here for a couple of weeks. But I look real skeptically at Carl. But Carl just shrugs as if saying well it's their asses, and it is, and Charlie and Jack don't seem concerned. But I don't like it one damn bit, and hopefully they won't take our asses down when they go down. Then the four of us go to the supermarket and get all the groceries for the trip. Then we come back to Jack's and divide the dry box things and the iced in coolers things that they will carry, and the dry box things and the iced in cooler things that we will carry. Then we all agree to meet at Casper's at three thirty in the morning. Then for a few minutes we just stand around with big smiles on our faces and looking excited like we are kids on the last day of school and have the whole summer before us.

Then Carl and I go by my apartment and gather the gear there and take it down to my skiff. And for the next hour we sort and pack and load. Then finally there isn't anything more to do. But we continue leaning against my skiff and looking in at all the stowed gear with silly grins on our faces because tomorrow we go to Ocracoke. Finally Carl reluctantly says, "well, so, I'll see you at three thirty." And I say, yeah, great, see you then. And we shake hands, which is something we hardly ever do, but seems to be the appropriate thing to do now. Then Carl leaves. And I look up the hill and see that all the cars are gone except Jennifer's. All the people are returning to their inland homes. Soon Jennifer will start for Greensboro. Their weekend at the coast over. And I already feel the void of Jennifer gone. And I feel the rush of the same old helplessness and hopelessness. It never gets easier. It always gets harder. But Jennifer will appear again, next week, next month, sometime. She always does. But that doesn't ease the hurt now one damn bit.

So I walk across the gravel yard to where Oscar Schneider is sitting leaning with both hands on his cane on the bench in front of Casper's. The weekenders are gone from around here too. So Swansboro is ours again until next weekend. But Oscar just continues looking across the Waterway and the marshes to Bear Islands's backside dunes as I sit down beside him. And I know that in his mind he is gone fishing on some trip that happened years before. Because that is what old fishermen do. They have only to look across the water then right away they are gone fishing in their minds on some trip that happened years before. And the older they get the longer they sit on benches and the further forward they lean with both hands on their canes and the more they are gone fishing in their minds. Because that is what old fishermen do.

"About ready?" Oscar asks quietly still looking across the water.

"Yessir, about."

"Watch northeast and southwest up there. If anything builds it will come from one or the other. If it comes and the wind stays one or the other, fine, just another storm. But if it comes then the wind starts to back around counter clockwise, Keith, you haul ass in somewhere fast. Because it's about to get sure enough bad, and it'll be around for awhile."

So I say, yessir I will, and I look at his stomped on looking hard old fisherman's hands and at his ever squinting leatherly old fisherman's face, and I know what I already have begun to look like.

Then he says even more quietly, "it's true you know she really doesn't care up there." But he says this matter of factly, like an experienced traveler advising an inexperienced traveler of a potentially rough stretch of road ahead. Wormshoes's warning came from a scare from a situation that he didn't take the time to understand, that happened up there. And Larry has never been up there, though he has been on the edges of similar waters, so his warning was just the customary one that fishermen give each other before a trip. But Oscar goes back to when they still haul-seined mullet in rowed surf boats from the beach at Bear Island then salted them in wood barrels. Oscar damn well knows.

So I say that I'm watching the forecasts carefully, but so far nothing unusual is coming. But he brings his face from looking across the water and looks at me real sternly and says for me to forget about forecasts. That they

won't tell me nature's signs that say when not to leave the dock at all, and when to stop fishing and come in fast before something sure enough bad happens.

That those signs are what the fishermen up there know that I don't know. That down here there are plenty of places to hide after something happens, that they don't have up there. That this is the next thing I have to learn if I am to be the fisherman that they are up there. But I am stunned, because I didn't know that we down here aren't the fishermen that they are up there. But Oscar wouldn't say it if it wasn't so. Then he looks back across the water and says quietly again, "I had to learn the signs the hard way, and that's how you need to learn them so you won't forget them." And I can tell by his eyes that he is gone fishing again on some trip that happened years before when a storm begins to build usual enough.

But this time it just keeps building and worsening and worsening until the Pamlico Sound becomes a truly terrible place to be in a boat. Until just finding the channel between all the blunt raw shoals is impossible, much less running to a somewhere safe harbor. With solid foamy spray bursting from the bow and smashing against the windshield until the glass groans. Until the propeller screams its spinning and cannot catch. Until the below engine thunders its helplessness. Until the boat scuds wildly across the swells and wallows heavily through the troughs, and visibility becomes zero and the compass swings crazily. And the just thrown anchor to keep her bow to only bumps along the bottom uselessly. And the just thrown sea anchor to keep her bow to only barely slows her backward racing toward the everywhere around blunt raw shoals. Until Oscar Schneider learns something the hard way.

Then his eyes slowly stop looking across the water, and his hands on the cane stop the twitching that they had started, and he quietly asks, "so, have you given any more thought to buying the 'Secret Woman?'" But I am still stunned by what I had seen in his far away up there eyes just now. So I say the first thing I can think of. "She's a fine trawler, Oscar, she really is."

And he nods his agreement. "Built her Harkers Island style thirty years ago this fall. Harkers Island is the only style for fishing this coast. Spent a week up there with the Willis brothers designing her in my mind and arranging for the lumber and watching how they cut this and how they shape that. Built her right here at Casper's, that was back when old man Bill Casper was still alive. On blocks right over there where the gravel ends." And he points with a stomped on looking old fisherman's hand. "She's as tight today as the day she was launched, but you know that. Fished her so much the wife swore I had another woman, but the 'Secret Woman' was my only other woman." And he smiles as he remembers. "Fished her all along this coast until several years ago when I got so I just couldn't. Always figured Oscar Jr. would take up where I left off. But he likes that every Friday paycheck too much, and you can't blame him for that. But fishing was all we had back then, all we wanted really. None of us had a regular job. And wouldn't have taken one anyway. But times change. But I'll let the worms have her before I see her not fishing, and that's a fact. Told Oscar Jr. so to his face. He wants her for weekend rides,for the grandkids, but I'll let the worms have her first. She's too proud to end up as a weekend rides boat for kids." Then he looks at me steadily and his eyes soften. "Keith, you're the only one of this bunch here that I'd let have her."

"Well, I appreciate that, Oscar, I do." And I do, because I know how big a compliment that is coming from him. "But you know how bad clamming is. So ten thousand is all the money in the world to me. But that is a mighty fair price, it sure is." But I'm hedging, even though ten thousand really is all the money in the world to me right now. Because my skiff and outboard and trailer are not a big investment. I can park them in my yard and go do something else anytime things get really bad and stay that way. But owning the 'Secret Woman' would be a long term commitment to fishing it really would. I could not park her and walk away from her, the investment and the responsibility would be just too great. But the coastal development will not stop. And the over fishing will not stop. And the pollution will not stop. So all the fisheries here can only continue to shrink until finally they are dead. So, yes, I'm hedging.

"I'll get to the money in a minute." He says with a small wave of his hand. "Keith, Carl would be next after you. But Carl's a clammer. He's a damn good one, and a real hard worker. But he only wants to clam, he doesn't want to be a fisherman. You do, everyone can see that. But the future has you scared. Keith, gas engine were supposed to kill fishing when they took over from sails. And digging the Waterway there was supposed to kill fishing when they joined all the inland waters. And the list goes on and on. There were years when the shrimp simply didn't show. up. There were years when the fish simply didn't show up. And everyone said fishing was over with, fishing was dead. But we kept fishing, and we got by somehow. Through the no market years, through the many hurricane years, we just kept fishing. Keith, there have always been fisherman along this coast, and there always will be. And there always will be ten reasons why you can't do something, to only one reason why you can. But through it all you just keep fishing. Why? Because you're a fisherman. Fishermen, fish. That's all they know to do. That's all they want to do."

Then he stops talking to give all that a minute to sink in. And I sit here and know that all I have to do is say yes and the 'Secret

Woman' is mine. That truly beautiful twenty five foot trawler, rigged so one man can work her, with all of her gear so all of the fisheries would be open to me. And I sit here and know that no decision has ever scared me so much.

Then Oscar says, "put one thousand down, pay me a thousand a year. No interest, no paper, we shake hands in front of Oscar Jr. so he knows the deal. I die, you pay him. You take care of her like I would. That's the deal." And he thumps his cane end in the gravel to settle it.

So I sit here torn between whether to hug Oscar thank you, thank you, or to run up the hill to my apartment as fast as I can to get away from him. Yes, there is no greater compliment than this deal to how hard I've worked and how hard I've tried to learn fishing these past five years. But that doesn't change how terrible the future does look for fishermen. So I say, "Oscar let me make this trip to Ocracoke. We'll talk when I get back." And he says that sounds fair enough. But I'm still hedging. But I've already made my decision.

CHAPTER EIGHT

I have the navigational chart for Ocracoke south to Core Sound and to just past Atlantic and Sealevel spread out on my kitchen table. The apartment is hushed with the night sounds of solitude. I am standing leaning over the chart with one leg up and my foot on a kitchen chair and a forearm resting on that knee with a beer in one hand and cigarette in the other hand. And I slowly look at all the familiar landmarks. I am familiarizing myself with the familiar. There is Teach's Hole where Blackbeard got caught and killed by the British, just outside of Ocracoke harbor toward the Inlet. There is the old old town of Portsmouth and then Portsmouth Island that becomes Core Banks further south. There is North Rock and Shell Castle and Ayers Rock and Beacon Island west and a little south of Ocracoke Inlet and out in the middle of everything. Then west of them is Royal Shoal sticking out into Pamlico Sound like a huge question mark, with four feet of water at low tide here, and two feet at low tide there, then one foot then three feet, then two and two, several fives, another four, a three. Yeah, Royal Shoal is a widow maker to the big trawlers for sure. All of this up here is. Lots of shoals. Lots and lots of shoals. So I stand here and see it all in my mind as if I were right there looking at it, and it all feels as comfortable as home. Hodges Reef there behind Portsmouth Island, all ones and twos at low so skiffs can't even navigate there. Then south is Mullet Shoal which is completely out at low and a good place to get stranded until high if you don't watch out. Then to the west is Shell Island named because it is all shells obviously. You clammed there, when? Uh, two years ago this past spring, yes. Then Wainwright Island named for some fella named Wainwright I guess. Then Harbor Island, probably was a staging harbor there for the old sailing ships hauling coastal freight. Then Chain Shot Island, funny name, wonder where that came from, I don't know. Then Hog Island, guess it had some wild pigs on it way back. And all of this is where Core Sound ends and Pamlico Sound begins, or Core Sound begins and Pamlico ends, depending on the direction you're coming from. There's Lola on the south east end of Cedar Island. Dear Lola. I went to visit Lola one day, but Lola isn't there anymore. Use to be a village of living people, now just a dot and a name on a navigational chart. Lola, a cluster of frame homes around a fish dock and a jot-um-down store beside the water,that is no more. Wonder who Lola was? Most likely a fisherman's wife. Wonder whether she was tall or short, fair or dark? Lola, dear sweet Lola. And he loved her so much he named the village for her as a tribute to her loveliness. So when he was gone fishing and said well it's time to go home to Lola, he damn well meant it. Lola, you are so fine, so good, so beautiful and I love you so that I have decided to live always within you. Must have been one hell of a lady, our Lola, standing on the dock looking far across the water for her fisherman. Her long skirt blowing in the wind, one hand shading her eyes against the setting sun. But she is long dead now, just as they all are long dead, and their village also. But before this, Lola got her name and her dot on a navigational chart, so Lola will never die now. Lola lives. Lola, sweet Lola. Well, it's almost nine, finish this beer then go to bed, two thirty will come mighty early. Okay, in a minute. Here south of Cedar Island is Thorofare Bay where we worked the clam dredge for several days last winter in a screaming northeaster of six to eight foot swells. And it was several days after that before the all day throbbing of the engines and the endless hard slamming of the dredge finally left you. Then south, Atlantic then Sealevel that look across Core Sound to Core Banks. So I stand here and see it all in my mind as if I were right there looking at it, and it all feels as comfortable as home. Go to bed. Okay, just one more minute. So I look back up to Shell Castle and see all of the shoals that are between it and Ocracoke harbor. Lots of two feet, one foot, three feet at low. Lots and lots. But low tide up there tomorrow will be early morning, and we will cross tomorrow afternoon. So there will be plenty of water on the shoals for a straight shot across in the skiffs. If in doubt just follow the crab trap floats because crabbers always set their traps in the deepest water. But there should be plenty of water. But it's better to be safe than sorry.

Then Jennifer says, "Keith!" from the living room. And I say. "Yeah! Back here." But I think, 'what the hell is she doing here?!' Then I realize that this is the first time I have ever resented Jennifer's coming. Ever. Because in my mind I am already gone to

Shell Castle, and she is intruding on that.

She walks in with a scotch in one hand and a two thirds full fifth and her cigarettes and her lighter in the other hand, and I think, 'god damn she's come for the night.' Then I see how flat her eyes are and how narrow her lips are, and I think, 'and she's come to fight.' But I say, "I thought you left for Greensboro."

"Robert rode with friends, I'll go back tomorrow, " and she bites off each word. So I straighten from leaning over the chart and just look at her while she glares at me. And I think, 'here it comes.' Then in a rush she says, "so what the hell did you do to Billie yesterday?"

So I get a snapped back expression of surprise on my face and say, "I didn't do anything to Billie."

Then her words start tumbling out. "Well, she came in from clamming yesterday afternoon, hardly said anything to anyone, took a shower, ate a little bit, then went to bed. When I got up this morning she had left for Charlotte, left a note saying she wanted to beat the traffic. Robert said he heard her leave about seven thirty."

But none of this sounds that unusual. Not enough to get Jennifer this bent out of shape. "All day on the water just knocked her out, Jennifer. She was done in, so she went to bed early. And you can't blame her for wanting to beat the traffic. Maybe she wanted to prepare something special for her science class tomorrow."

"Lunch today was the yearly get together of a bunch of our college friends, Keith. We had been planning it for months. That's the reason Billie came down this weekend, the only reason." And she stands there glaring at me like Billie and I have something going and she is hiding here until everyone has left.

But I've already had it with this kind of attitude. "Well, I don't know anything about that. We had a real nice day on the water, that's all I know. Look, the phone's in the living room, Jennifer, call her and ask her about this yourself. And why don't you put those things down before you drop them?"Then she looks down and sees her hands still full, and she puts everything on the table.

Then a flash gets into her flat eyes, and she jams her hands on her hips and says, "and Robert is very upset with you for not coming over last night to talk with him about the seafood market like you said you would!"

"Look Jennifer, you better tone this down and fast. Or I'll have your ass out the back door and bouncing across the lawn in a heart beat." And I mean it because now I'm pissed.

"You put one hand on me and Robert ---"

"And Robert will do what?! Robert won't do shit! I'd have his ass stomped so fast it would make his head swim. Then send him going down the road blubbering like a whipped kid. Robert ain't shit! I've been fucking you for years with him home asleep in the next block. Robert's a pussy, Jennifer! What will Robert do? Robert won't do shit!"

So her mouth flies open and her jaw falls down and her eyes get wide and her face drains white. Then she starts sputtering and stuttering like Wormshoe, "Well, I never, Robert, well, how dare,

Keith, never, well---"

"Just drop it, Jennifer! Just get the hell out! I'm leaving for Ocracoke in several hours, and I certainly don't need this."

"My but aren't we the forceful one all of a sudden?" Her having almost recovered. This being the first time I have ever seen her flustered.

"Maybe I've always been, but you didn't notice. Or maybe I was so afraid of making you mad and losing one night with you that I really didn't show it. But either way here it is, this is me, like it or not, take it or leave it." And I notice that we are panting from all the emotions. So I take a drink of beer and I see that my hand is shaking badly. Then she takes a drink of scotch and I see that her hand is shaking badly.

Then suddenly we are in each others arms and grabbing and kissing and holding. Then we are going down the hall and into the bedroom and we are tearing off each other's clothes and into bed. Normally we have a long slow tender climb together of her coming twice then I come, then rest and a drink and a cigarette, then a second long slow tender climb together, then sleep. But now I decide that I simply will not come, and I begin to pound her hard. I pound and pound and pound and she comes and comes and comes, but then she stops coming but I keep pounding and pounding and I feel her begin to get dry inside, but I keep pounding and finally she is whimpering, "Keith, please, no, Keith, it hurts baby, please." But I keep pounding because I want her to hurt too because I am tired of living alone with the endless hurt of Jennifer,

Jennifer.

Now I am sitting with a beer in the plaid chair in the living room. The late night sounds of the waterfront come up from Casper's on a light wind through the open windows. A disturbed heron begins to fuss in the distance. And I am remembering that I have had many personal shortcomings and failures so far in my life. But that these are the usual baggage of life, so I have accepted them and I carry them as easily as I can. But I have always tried to be very careful to never do anything that I would be ashamed of. Because shame is needless baggage, shame can be crippling baggage. And there is plenty of baggage without that baggage. But just now I acquired some of that baggage, that excess baggage, that shame baggage. So I sit here not liking myself at all. Then I hear her leave the bathroom and go to the kitchen and mix a drink.

Now she is sitting in the flowered chair sipping the scotch. Her eyes are puffy and red from crying. So now I feel hate for myself.

"I'm sorry, Jennifer." And I want to reach across and hold her hand, but I don't.

"Maybe some of the blame is mine."

"That can't excuse what I did."

"Keith, I'm not always the nice person you think I am." And again there is the huskiness in her voice and her perfume and her black shimmering hair.

"That can't excuse me either." But somehow I have never

been able to see her as a person, the way I can clearly see other people as people. Somehow she is always Jennifer, Jennifer's somewhere up there on a pedestal.

"Well, it's over, so we will forget it."

But I know we won't. I know I can't. So we do not say anything for several minutes. Then down along the waterfront the disturbed heron squawks irritably and loses patience and I can hear its huge wings beat as it rises in flight.

"Keith, Robert really is upset with you for not coming over last night."

"Jennifer, you know I am a fisherman. You know I am not a manager of a seafood market."

"But you can learn to be. Don't you want to better yourself?"

And suddenly the anger is here again. But I quickly push it back and say, "there isn't anything wrong with being a fisherman, Jennifer."

"No. But you can be more."

"I only want to be a very good fisherman. And that is a lot to want to be."

"Honestly, you can be so hardheaded sometimes. Keith, Robert has to be things he doesn't want to be in order to get ahead. There isn't anything wrong with that. At times we all have to compromise."

Now the anger is boiling, it is. Because what Robert does doesn't have anything to do with what I do. But still she wants me to be like Robert. But there's no way in hell that I will ever be a mild-mannered packaged man. But I don't want to make her mad. Because I don't want her to leave. So now I'm doing it again. I'm letting how very different she and I are slide, simply because I don't want her to leave. The clear forcefulness has left me. So now I don't like myself for another reason. Now I don't know which way to go with the conversation. She will nail me to the wall if I don't think carefully before I speak. But I am confused by all of tonight's emotions. And the anger is boiling, it is, and I have to say something. So I lash out and say anything, "you god damn people come down here and buy up the coast, then bring your friends and crowd us out." But right away I know that that doesn't have anything to do with what we are talking about. Right away I know that that is another frustration, that doesn't

that doesn't have anything to do with this my frustration of Jennifer.

Her eyebrows go up as she sips scotch. "You people? Who is, 'you people,' Keith?" Then she looks at me and gently says, "Keith, we have as much right to be down here as you do."

And she is right. And she only gently nails me to the wall. Because I am mixing frustrations. But there is really only one frustration. And I have to say it finally. So I say, "Jennifer, I want to marry you."

And her eyebrows go up again. "But I'm already married, silly."

"Divorce Robert. Marry Me."

"Oh really, Keith, you take everything so seriously."

"Y'all have a business arrangement, Jennifer, not a

marriage."

"But it works for us, Keith. No, we don't sleep together. But we are friends. We really do fit, however it may look to everyone else."

"Do you love me?"

"Yes." And I can see in her eyes that she does.

"Then marry me, Jennifer."

"Oh Keith, you can be so silly sometimes."

I am still awake when the alarm goes off, and I hit the button before Jennifer wakes. Her face is on my chest and her arm is across me and her breathing is a whisper. I ease her over on to her back but right away she curls on her side with her hands close to her face and her mouth in a pout. Now I am dressed and ready to go. So I lean down and brush back the black black hair from her face and I softly kiss her on the cheek. Her perfume is everywhere once again, and I know that I will never be able to get away from it. So me and my recently acquired shame walk out into the hall.

CHAPTER NINE

As I walk down the grassy hill to Casper's I see Carl under the tall yard lights as he hooks onto my trailer and skiff. Then as I walk up to him he is plugging in the trailer lights connection.

"Morning, Carl."

"Good morning, Keith." And he looks at me and says, "god, you look like death warmed over."

"And I feel the same way."

"That Greensboro woman again?"

"That Greensboro woman again."

"That ain't healthy, Keith, and you know it. Find yourself a nice girl and get married. You're killing yourself this way."

"You won't get an argument from me about that."

"Well, go stand behind the trailer and tell me if the lights work, okay?"

"Okay." And I go stand behind the trailer.

He says running lights and I say yeah. He says left turn and I say yeah. He says right turn and I say yeah. He says brake and I say yeah. Then he says all set. Then Jack drives up with Charlie, pulling Charlies's skiff. We can hear Charlie talking loud here in the early morning quiet. "I'm going to beat you so bad clamming you won't show your face in Swansboro again. Why I'll make you look so bad you'll go inland and do pulpwood work, that's how bad I'm going to beat you." Then Jack answers. "Yeah? Yeah? Think so huh? Well, we'll just see about that. Why I was already clamming when you were still sucking your mother's tit." Then Charlie. "Yeah? Is that right? Think so huh? We'll see. We'll just see about that."

So Carl says they're already at it and I answer yeah. Then we say good morning to them, and they say good morning to us. Then Carl asks them if they are ready, and they answer yeah. Then Charlie starts saying how he is going to beat Jack so bad clamming that he will never show his butt ugly face around Swansboro again. And Jack starts answering yeah, yeah, think so huh? But I don't want to hear it anymore, so I walk around and get in Carl's truck.

Then Carl gets in and says, "they're a hell of a pair to spend four days on a marsh island with."

"They're god damn idiots."

"Well, too late now. You ready?"

"I'm ready."

"We forget anything?"

"If we did, we'll do without it."

"Okay, Ocracoke here we come."

"I'm' with you, Carl."

Then we pull out of Casper's gravel yard and onto the street and Swansboro is dark and quiet as we pass. I turn and see Jack and Charlie pull out too. So we really are on our way. But my eyelids   are   already   heavy and I can hardly hold my head up. Now Carl has us out of Swansboro and crossing the bridges over the White Oak River and heading for Morehead City. So I settle in the seat and put my head back and then nothingness. Morehead City's street lights almost wake me as we pass under them light, dark, light, dark. Then we are stopped at the convenience store where we take a hard right going to Otway and Williston and Davis and Stacy, then Sealevel and Atlantic and Cedar Island. Carl asks me if I want coffee, and I grunt no. Then nothingness again. And soon the gentle swaying of my head on the seat back resumes.

I awake when Carl shuts off the truck. I see that we are in line for the ferry at the landing on Cedar Island. Cars and cars pulling campers and motor homes are lined up. The sun comes over the horizon and starts its climb. But now the water across to Core Banks is all bright light and I cannot look at it.

"Feel Better?"

"Some." But now I feel worse than death warmed over.

"Let's have breakfast. There's plenty of time."

"Okay."

So the four of us walk across the parking areas to the restaurant. Charlie starts in about Jack's falling asleep and running off the road several times and scaring the shit out of him. But Jack swears it was just the narrow curvy road, and how did Charlie know anyway since he was asleep the whole trip? But I just tune them out, and concentrate on not dying. There is a full breakfast buffet spread out inside the restaurant. When I see it steaming and it's smelling so good, I suddenly realize how hungry I am, half starved even. So I pile a plate with scrambled eggs and hash browns and link sausage and cantaloupe and biscuits, and eat the whole damn thing. Because I treat myself special whenever I can.

The big diesels really start throbbing to get the loaded ferry safely pulled away from the landing in the strong current that runs there. There isn't anything but the huge open Pamlico Sound ahead. The sun is higher, but still very bright. The heat and the humidity are already building. The vehicles are side by side and end to end close together with only walking room between. People start getting out and stretching and going to the rails to see better. And strangers begin talking excitedly with strangers. Seagulls start their hovering and bitching and begging for food. These are in their job descriptions, and they take their jobs seriously. But I lean my head back on the seat and go to sleep to the steady throb of the diesels now that we are well away from the landing and underway. I am full, and I feel better, but just one more hour of sleep, please.

But I dream a fragmented weird dream of Wormshoe waltzing with Billie Griffin at Sammy's while Larry plays the accordion and stamps his foot while I dance pirouettes down the long bar while Carl juggles three pool balls and sings It's A Rainy Night In Georgia.

I awake to Carl's talking with a tourist fellow who is standing beside the truck. Carl is saying that clamming is feast or famine, good week bad week, like any other kind of commercial fishing. The fellow says that he knew guys could make a living shrimping or fishing, but he didn't know guys could make a living clamming. So Carl says, sometimes we can and sometimes we can't. So the fellow says that he could tell by our boats and our stuff that we weren't going weekend fishing. And Carl says no, that we are going to our jobs just like he goes to his job. So the fellow starts telling Carl how he has an office supply store in Greenville, South Carolina. And how he brings the wife and kids up to Kitty Hawk every summer this time because of how isolated it is there. But I have seen how wall to wall that Kitty Hawk has developed and I wonder how he can call that isolated, but compared to Greenville I guess it is. But now I can tell that Carl is just about talked out, him not being much of a long winded talker anyway. But the fellow is just getting started. So the fella starts in about how they are all shellers and birders, the kids too, which I guess means that they collect shells and they watch birds. But now Carl gets real fidgety, him not being that comfortable around tourists anyway, and I am afraid he might sling an arm out the truck window and sprawl this fellow on the deck. So I say, "want a beer, Carl?" And Carl looks at me like I have just dropped down from heaven.

"Uh, yeah. But the sign there says no smoking, no alcoholic beverages."

"Didn't ask you what the sign says, asked if you want a beer?" So Carl smiles and nods. Meanwhile, the tourist fellow has us tip toe creeping through the bush in hot pursuit of a blue bill red chested forked tailed brown throated yellow warbler with a purple crown, or some such.

So I get out of the truck and start feeling around in an iced cooler in back. And I ask, "you want a beer, fella?", to stop the tourists from his now runaway rattling on. Because even though I feel much better, I have already enjoyed about as much of his rattling on as I can stand. And he stops in midsentence and says thanks but no thanks. But thankfully right at this moment his wife hollers to him that the kids want to go feed the seagulls. So now it is the tourist's turn to get fidgety, and he quickly says to Carl that maybe they can talk more later before we land, but for now the little woman has spoken.. So I stand here and wonder why one tourist will avoid us like the plague, while the next will pester us mercilessly. Then I look back towards the ferry's stern, and sure enough there are the gulls hovering and bitching and begging like always. Ospreys earn their food with skill and work, pelicans too, black skimmers too. In fact all the shorebirds earn their food with skill and work, except gulls. Gulls are bums and thieves and scavengers. But the shore needs a sanitation department, and the gulls are it. But god damn they are always so bitchy.

So Carl and I are enjoying our beers and cigarettes and being out of the now hard sun for awhile, when one of the ferry's young deckhands walks up.

"Y'all keep the beer and cigarettes down, okay? The Captain's a real shit about that. But he won't leave the bridge, and he can't see you if you stay in the truck."

"Okay, thanks." Both Carl and I say.

"Where y'all going clamming?"

"Shell Castle." Carl says.

"Should do pretty well. Not many clam there. I'm from Sealevel. I pearake behind Core Banks on my days off. Where y'all from?"

"Swansboro." I say.

"Hear y'all are good clammers down there."

"We try." Carl says.

"The buyer in Atlantic, Joe Gaskill, is paying eleven, if that beats your buyer's price."

"Sure does," I say, "he's paying ten."

"Well, Joe's just getting started, and he'll appreciate the business. Better go check on the other passengers. Just keep it down and no one will bother you, okay?"

So we both say okay, and he walks on towards the stern, and Carl says nice fella and I agree. Then on my side of the truck, I see Charlie and Jack walking between vehicles coming back for the bow. They see two girls in a top down convertible, and head straight for them. "Charlie and Jack just zeroed in on two girls in a convertible, Carl."

"Good, that'll keep them occupied for awhile."

Then after a moment I say, "Carl, I'm going to buy the 'Secret Woman' from Oscar Schneider."

And Carl whistles air and says, "that's a big step, Keith, you sure you want to take it?"

"Well, I'm just marking time the way I'm going. It's time for me to either go ahead and become a fisherman, or go do something else. Because we won't be able to clam full-time for very much longer."

"Well, she's a mighty fine trawler, there's no doubting that. But a big responsibility also."

"Carl, I'll probably move somewhere up here too. I can work more different fisheries with her up here. And somehow up here feels like home, it's hard to explain."

"When you do make a decision, you don't mess around."

"Well, it isn't definite. But I'm leaning that way."

"Well, I'll sure miss the hell out of you, if you do move up here. That's for sure."

And in my mind 'Secret Woman' and I are planed off nicely and running smoothly in fair weather by Chain Shot Island and with Harbor Island ahead, then Wainwright Island, and in the distance is Pamlicio Sound. Then I see Charlie coming quickly between the vehicles towards us.

"We found a couple of babes up there in a convertible." He says a little breathlessly. "They're staying tonight in Ocracoke. Let's stay over too, then get a real early start for Shell Castle in the morning."

"No Charlie," I say, "we came to clam, not to mess with girls."

"Ah man, come on, what's one night?"

"We will get there this afternoon in time to clam several hours after we get the camp set up. And get started fresh in the morning without a five mile boat ride first."

"Ah man, come on. What do you think, Carl?"

"Keith's right, we came to clam."

"Ah man, shit." And Charlie sounds like someone had just licked his lollipop. "Well, Jack and I may stay over anyway, and come out in the morning. Hell with y'all."

"Suit yourselves," I say. Then Charlie is going back between the vehicles like he is a little boy kicking up dirt in disgust.

So Carl and I sit here and finish our beers and don't say anything. But we are both thinking the same thing.

Now Carl and I are parked in the shady picnic area beside the ferry landing at Ocracoke. We are sitting on the truck tailgate and between us is the fried chicken and potato salad and pickles and biscuits and sweet tea that Sara had fixed. The ferry is already loaded again, and its diesels have started their heavy throbbing before pulling away from the landing. Everyone who came with us made a beeline around the harbor to Ocracoke village as soon as we landed, Jack and Charlie in fast pursuit of the two girls in the convertible also. Some of the tourists will sight see for several hours, then continue north. Others will stay the night, then continue north. But most continued north for Hatteras as soon as we landed. This is Ocracoke from spring to summer until fall. Incoming and outgoing tidal surges of people and vehicles, broken only by brief sighs of relief. But in winter few come and few go, and the island fever becomes maddening and so very welcome to the Ocracokers. Carl and I are full and relaxed and thoroughly enjoying the shady quiet, when we see Jack and Charlie come back along the road and pull into the picnic area. We can see them arguing with each other before we can hear them.

"Well, I don't blame her for getting scared when you asked her what color her panties were, Charlie! Then bet that they were pink. Then dared her to show you to prove it. Then said she was chicken if she didn't. And you wouldn't shut up about her panties. You ain't got no couth, man! You shouldn't be allowed around people. No couth, man, no couth at all." And Jack is thoroughly disgusted.

"Hell, Jack, she laughed didn't she? She didn't mind. She laughed didn't she?"

"Yeah, then hauled ass around all the traffic, and left us standing flat footed beside the road. Hell, they're at the Hatteras ferry landing by now. We were in real good with them until you started drooling over the color of her panties, then wouldn't shut up about them. You shouldn't be allowed outside Swansboro, man, you give the rest of us a bad name."

"She laughed, didn't she? She didn't mind." But Charlies's protest is pretty lame by now.

So Carl says, "there's plenty of fried chicken and potato salad. Eat, then we'll launch the skiffs." So Jack and Charlie stand beside the tailgate and eat, with Jack looking thoroughly disgusted and Charlie looking pretty lame.

Now the skiffs are loosely tied to the dock beside the launching ramp. All the gear from the trucks has been transferred to the skiffs and properly stowed. The trucks and boat trailers are across the street in a parking area. The iced coolers have been drained and reiced. The store that is built on pilings beside the dock has some of everything from fishing tackle to food to drinks to medical supplies to softback books and magazines to camping gear to outboard motor parts and so forth that are stacked and rowed and trayed and boxed everywhere through out the cramped room. The owner has the red streaked eyes and the leathery face and the gnarled hands of a long time fisherman. Whenever he can, he sits one cheeked on a stool behind the cash register with his left leg outstretched and resting. For the past hour he has kept track of our few purchases on a rumpled receipt book with a stubby pencil. Usually he just pointed to where the things were that we wanted, without stirring from the stool. Now he has everything totaled and I pay for it and I put the receipt in my shirt pocket so I can settle with the others later.

"Clammers?"

"Yessir. Going to Shell Castle for several days."

"Might should think about coming in tomorrow, what with the sun dogs."

I don't know what sun dogs are, so I say, "we've been following the forecasts closely."

"Well, might should think about coming in tomorrow anyway, what with the sun dogs."

So I say okay and I thank him and when I get outside I look at the sun without looking directly at it. But other than a slight halo hazy around it, it just looks bright as hell and feels hot as hell. Carl is standing in the bow of my skiff waiting for me to get in so he can untie and shove off. "What's a sun dog, Carl?" But he says he doesn't know. So I look indirectly at the sun again, then shrug and get in my skiff and Carl shoves off the bow.

We run slow without wakes down the harbor, Carl and I ahead and Jack and Charlie behind, with our skiffs setting a little low in the water with all the gear but not too much so. Ocracoke village is behind now, and we pass the picnic area and the ferry landing. The Coast Guard Station is ahead on the right, and several guardsmen are cleaning one of their launches at their dock. As we pass, one of them hollers, "where y'all headed?" and Carl hollers, "Shell Castle", and the guardsman waves his hand that he heard. Then we pass through the narrow harbor entrance with the big boulder breakwaters on either side. Then, ahead suddenly and all around is Ocracoke Inlet wide and huge and shining to the far distance. I purposely did not go to the rail to see this view as we approached Ocracoke on the ferry. Because I wanted to run slow coming down the harbor so the anticipation could build and build gradually. Then for the view to again suddenly explode open from skiff level on my own terms in my own time privately and personally. Like seeing home again. Like coming around a blind bend, and suddenly there it is, home! Long lost and now found again, home. Portsmouth Island over there, low and dark and almost far away. The Inlet itself to the left, angry at the either side beaches with the shoals in front. And the mighty Atlantic huge beyond them. Shell Castle due south ahead, but still too low to be seen but there none the less. Pamlico Sound to the right, with it's own special yawning hugeness and sometimes anger. Yes, like coming passed the breakwaters, and suddenly there is home.

"There's Teach's Hole, Carl! See it? Blackbeard's Hole! See it there?" And I point left to the big cove before the Inlet at Ocracoke's southern shore. And Carl briefly looks and barely nods, because I make him suffer this every time we go to Shell Castle. "The Portsmouth traders were badly undercutting the Virginia traders for the West Indies trade. So a British warship was sent down to sack Portsmouth in November of seventeen eighteen. But when the warship came through the Inlet at dawn, the many sailing vessels in Portsmouth harbor were just too formidable. So they looked around for something easier, and there was poor Blackbeard at anchor in that cove with everyone onboard asleep. So the gutless British attacked and he never stood a chance. They cut off his head and stuck it on their bowsprit and paraded that around awhile before they left. But Blackbeard wasn't much worse than most of them back then. Piracy was pretty much a way of life. Damn little law here then. But Blackbeard got the notoriety. But he wasn't any worse than most, not really. So they named it Teach's Hole. See it there, Carl?" And again Carl briefly looks and barely nods. "Probably not a bad sort, Carl, not really. Cruelty was pretty much everyday back then. Seventeen eighteen it was. That was two hundred and sixty seven years ago, Carl! Can you imagine that?" But in my mind I can see it as though it is happening right now. The British attacking, Blackbeard a sitting duck asleep. They kill him and cut off his head and stick it on their bowsprit and parade around here with it for awhile. "Right there, Carl, that happened right there!"

So we are planed off and running smoothly due south in an easy breeze. With high tide there is plenty of water on the shoals, so I stop following the crab trap floats. The shoals pass fast white under my skiff, and the water is so clear that I can see the seashells scattered in tiderows on them. Then ahead Beacon Island becomes a thin line that quickly thickens and darkens.

"That's Beacon Island ahead." I say to Carl above the outboard motor noise. "Or what's left of it. Storms have pretty well flattened it. Shell Castle is behind it. Should start seeing it soon. Alexander Hamilton had a fifty-foot light built on Beacon Island in seventeen ninety nine when he was Secretary of the Treasury. And so it's name." And Carl barely nods as he patiently continues to suffer through my rattling on. "Can you imagine that, Carl, a light fifty feet in the air right there? Why I bet you could see it for fifty miles in every direction. Well, maybe not that far, but a long god damn way anyway. A fifty-foot light right there, Carl, rising stark out of nothing but water everywhere to the horizon. Man, that had to absolutely dominate their world back then. That was a hundred and eighty six years ago, Carl. Can you imagine that? Hell, it would absolutely dominate our world now if it were there. At night it would be like god with a big flashlight looking around to see who's doing what. And everyone hiding and hoping like hell he isn't looking for them. Huh, Carl?"

Now we are running slow as we close on the western side of

Shell Castle and get ready to land. Our wake catches up with us and slides under the skiff playfully rocking it. Carl is standing in the bow with the bowline in his hand, ready to step out when we bump the bank. And we are like friendly explorers about to reclaim a familiar island. We are at Shell Castle, finally, after all the talking and the planning. And Charlie and Jack are very excited too, as they close on the bank from a little behind and a little above us. This is the marsh grass side of Shell Castle. But the marsh grass is a dusty green, a tired green what with the endless everyday hard heat. The high shell banks side of Shell Castle is on the other side facing Portsmouth. The several hundred resident pelicans prefer those shell banks, so that is where they are. The system of narrow shell reefs that is shaped like a large several hundred yard on each side irregular box, comes out from Shell Castle on the side facing Ocracoke. Inside this reef enclosed large box is a shallow bay, and the big patches of eel grass in it show as a dark good green in the light breeze rippled water. This is the prime clamming area because it is the prime clam habitat. So we are finally here to claim Shell Castle again.

So our tents are up and they look good in the smooth clearing between the stretches of packed shells and the tall marsh grass. All of the gear has been brought from the skiffs, and it has been properly placed and properly organized. So our camp now looks like a proper camp. And we are having cold beer and are walking all around investigating and are talking all together, because we are all glad as hell to be here. It is almost four and the sun is well passed it's peak and in an hour or so it will begin it's closing with the Pamlico Sound at the far horizon. But with it's decent so far, the heat and the glare have eased considerably. And the first puffs of an evening sea breeze from Portsmouth have started. But if we go ahead and get started, we can get in several hours of clamming before dark.

So Carl and I are trying here for clams and trying there for clams about midway on the outside of the narrow reef box leg that faces Portsmouth. My skiff is staked off inside the shallow bay on the other side of this narrow reef. Charlie and Jack are trying here, trying there inside the bay but further out than we are. We are not going for quantity so much as we are familiarizing ourselves with where the patches and the veins of clams are most concentrated so we will know where to begin work tomorrow without a lot of looking around. Carl takes a pull with his bullrake, then hollers to me how many he gets with that pull. I move down the reef aways and take a pull and holler to Carl how many I get. Then Carl moves and pulls and hollers, and we go like this for awhile. Now I have moved off the reef some and am down in the waist deep water. Ahead I see an area of much darker blue water, and I know that this is a hole that the tidal currents have scoured out between the all around shoals. And I know that sometimes clams can be really concentrated in holes. So I approach the hole rim slow step by slow step carefully so I won't step into the hole before I can stop. Then I take a pull at the lip of the rim with my bullrake and I get fifty some clams.

"Carl, I found a hole, and I think it's packed!' I holler, and Carl waves that he heard.

So I step to the rim and take a pull over the rim and up the side of the hole, and there are almost seventy clams in this pull. Now I suddenly get really excited. "It's god damn packed, Carl, it's wall to wall clams! Come on over!"

"Get 'em, Keith, get'em!" And I know that Carl is glad for me. But I also know that he won't come over to clam the hole. Because whoever finds a wall to wall hole or patch or vein, it is his.

"There's plenty for both of us, Carl! Really, I mean it! Come on over!" And Carl probably will come over once the full blush and bloom of this great discovery has worn off some for me.

Now I am neck deep down the side of the hole, with my left leg braced out in front so I can't go deeper, and my right leg bent up the side of the hole to steady me. And I push the bullrake out and down as deep into the hole as it can go, and very very carefully I take a pull. Then I very carefully back myself up the side of the hole until I am back up over the rim. And when I carefully turn the bull rake over it is to the brim with clams. There has to be more than a hundred! In one pull, more than a hundred clams! The mother lode. A commercial clammers dream, the mother lode. "It's the mother lode, Carl, it's the god damn mother lode! I found the mother lode, Carl!" And Carl is smiling real big, and he is glad as hell for me.

There are only two frying pans, so Charlie and Jack are frying their T-bones the way they like them, then Carl and I will fry our T-bones the way we like them. I drop a whole stick of butter in the pot of corn that is steaming on the camp stove in the lantern light. Carl is using a closed cooler for a counter as he opens an iced can of pears for each of us. And I am trying very hard to not say any more about finding the mother lode. Because I have already rubbed it in a little too much. So Charlie and Jack are unusually quiet, and I know that they are eat up with jealousy. If we were in Swansboro where we didn't have to be together, I would rub it in mercilessly on those two assholes. But we still have a long three more days together ahead of us, so I am trying hard to keep my mouth shut. Carl, though, is genuinely happy for me. But then I knew he would be, so now I like Carl even more because he is who he is. And tomorrow morning Carl and I will work together during low tide, when we can get really deep into that mother lode hole. But supper tonight will be subdued when normally it would be noisy. But Carl and I grin shit eating grins sideways at each other now and then anyway.

It is only nine thirty, but we are quiet because we are tired. It has been a full day since two thirty this morning. With the seabreeze, our clothes dryed quickly while we fixed supper without our getting cold, but now a windbreaker feels good. The itchy feeling that comes with beard stubble has started. As has the unclean feeling that comes with dryed saltwater in your clothes and on your skin. But these will get a lot worse before they get better. We are seated cross legged on the smooth clearing in front of our tents in lantern light with coolers for backrests. And we are enjoying the iced beer. The beer tomorrow night will just be cool. And after that, warm. And tomorrow night will be the last fresh meat supper for awhile. So Jack trys to get the girls's panties thing started again with Charlie, but it quickly trails off into silence. So I tell Carl to remind me to thank Sara for the fried chicken and potato salad and he nods that he will and Charlie and Jack say yeah them too. Then Charlie starts telling how he won ten dollars at pool from a shrimper last week at a dollar a game, but we aren't listening.

The night sky up here is gigantic, it is, and it is all around overhead like a close blanket. But there are so many forests and so many development lights around Swansboro that the night sky there seems smaller somehow and faded. Like you are aware of it there, but you aren't really impressed by it. But the night sky up here is truly impressive all right, startling even, with the stars and the planets and the constellations in brilliant relief across a huge nearby blanket. So I remind myself that with buying the 'Secret Woman', I should take a course in celestial navigation. Then I wonder whether I can handle the math involved. Then I assure myself that with hard work I can. Then suddenly from nowhere I see Jennifer's face while it is twisted with pain,and I hear her whimper, 'please Keith, it hurts.' So I grimace inwardly and I clinch my teeth to dispel these. Because I have the rest of my life to relive that shame. But I like myself a lot tonight, and I have every reason to like myself a lot tonight. And I want this liking myself a lot tonight to continue. So I force myself to picture Billie Griffin there holding the seahorse in her cupped hands and looking up at me and saying, 'look, Keith, oh oh." And gradually the grimace and the clinched teeth ease. Then Carl yawns long and loud, and the rest of us laugh and say, "yeah, me too."

So I take a leak away from the camp on the rise of a small shell bank. Carl is in our tent spreading out his sleeping bag and getting things situated. And Jack and Charlie are stirring around in front of their tent and getting ready to do the same thing. And I am still liking myself a lot. Because getting two thousand clams in two hours is the best I have ever done, ever, and something like it use to be long before the over fishing started. But they only got several cents a clam back then, while I will get at least ten cents. So I made two hundred dollars in two hours at the most honest work there is, I found the clams, I dug the clams, so they are all my clams. And Carl and I will each be able to make two hundred at low tide in the morning before the hole is thinned down to where it is time to leave it alone until next year when the clams have had a chance to repopulate themselves. And I should be able to make at least another two hundred before we stop work late tomorrow afternoon. So that will be six hundred dollars total, less say a hundred for trip expenses. So that will be five hundred clear, which is half the down payment for 'Secret Woman'. And with luck and hard work and finding another mother lode even if it isn't quite as good, I could, I just might could clear over a thousand for the trip. Yeah, but don't count your chickens before they hatch, and don't spend your money until you make it. Because you have already learned that the hard way about fishing. So I stand here alone on the rise in the dark and the seabreeze and look all around and thoroughly enjoy liking myself a lot.

God, what a huge sky they have up here. Now you know just how insignificant you are so tiny here beneath it. Now you know the meaning of the word dome. Because this is one hell of a dome that they have up here. And there is the big glow of the lights of Ocracoke. Ocracoke stands out very clearly on the horizon all right. But there are only several lights there at what little is left of Portsmouth. But it didn't use to be this way. Not anything like it is now. Because in the early seventeen hundreds, when Ocracoke only had several lights, Portsmouth already was a notoriously lusty seaport of five hundred people. Which for this coast at that time was a major city. Because for a hundred years Portsmouth handled more tonnage a year than Norfolk or Charleston, usually combined. It dominated all right. But it was a gathering of sharp traders from everywhere out for only the dollar. No Mr. Nice Guy merchant business was conducted in Portsmouth. Timber and corn and tobacco and turpentine and whatever were traded for molasses and salt and rum and whatever. The constant shuttling of basic goods. From the mainland to Portsmouth, from Portsmouth to the West Indies, from the West Indies to England and Europe. Then the reverse shuttling of basic goods all the way back to the mainland over there across Pamlico Sound. Whatever would sell, anything for a dollar. But no Mr. Nice Guy merchant business though. Yeah, Portsmouth must have been one lusty city back then all right. Hell, it was so notorious that Blackbeard traded there only when he absolutely had to. He lived in Ocracoke and avoided Portsmouth just as all the locals did. But the British caught him at anchor asleep and cut off his head when they didn't have the guts to sack Portsmouth because Norfolk was jealous. A real rowdy boomtown all right. The activity always frantic around the wharves and the warehouses and the shipfitting yards. The constant come and go of sailing vessels of every size from everywhere. But Portsmouth harbor started out shoally as hell. Then the people cut the trees and their cattle ate the grass, and with nothing holding the sand in place, the wind promptly blew it into the harbor. So the difficult became the impossible. So Portsmouth gradually strangled itself to death. So they built wharves and warehouses here on Shell Castle, when they no longer could easily get to Portsmouth by water. So Shell Castle here must have become frantic in its own right, lusty in its own right. But that was two hundred and sixty some years ago. Now the shallow bay there where most of the island use to be is just ideal clam habitat for us today. And maybe the hole where I got two thousand clams use to have six feet of sand and shell on it with hogsheads of tobacco in a wharehouse on timbers on top of that. Because up here is in continual change, always has been, always will be. And what always was, can overnight quickly become, never will be again. Because the sea and the wind and the storms made up here. And they are continually relandscaping it to suit themselves to their own schedule. And we can take that or we can leave that, but we cannot change that.

And maybe one of my people was here back then. Maybe that is why up here feels so much like home. Maybe he wandered his way to the West Indies. Then wandered his way here and stayed to work the wharves and the warehouses. Then finally wandered his way to the mainland. Then others of us wandered our way inland. Then I wandered my way to Swansboro. Now I have wandered my way back here to Shell Castle. Maybe Lola on Cedar Island was my great, great Grandmother. Maybe that is why I can see her so clearly standing there on the dock, her long skirt blowing in the wind, one hand shading her eyes against the setting sun and looking far across the water for her fisherman. Maybe her great, great Granddaughter is there waiting for me now. I'll be home before long, lovely Lola.

CHAPTER TEN

There is enough gray light for us to fix breakfast without the lantern. We are stiff and cold in the damp air, and we do not have very much to say to each other. But we quickly drink one pot of coffee while a second pot is perking on the stove. Carl has the pound and a half of bacon done, so he drains the grease from the pan. Then he takes a spatula and crunches up the crisp bacon into small pieces. Meanwhile I have sixteen eggs scrambled in a bowl, and I salt and pepper them. So Carl puts the pan of crunched bacon back on the stove and I pour the eggs into it and right away the eggs begin to sputter and to steam. And Jack has four cans of chilled peaches open. And Charlie has a loaf of bread in several stacks on top of a cooler with an open jar of grape jam beside them. And the plates and the knives and forks and paper towels are laid out on top of another cooler.

Then the sun comes up from behind Portsmouth Island as we finish eating. But it brings with it a bunch of red that badly streaks the sky there.

So Charlie says, "red sky in the morning, sailors take warning."

"That means no wind." Carl says.

"No, means storm coming." Jack replies.

So right away we get into a short heated discussion of what

'red sky at night, sailors delight, red sky in the morning, sailors take warning,' means. I say that the saying came from the sail days, so it has to have to do with wind. But Jack insists again that it has to do with weather. And Carl agrees with me, but only half heartedly now. Then Charlie starts to say something, but doesn't. And I realize that I have heard that saying a thousand times, even long before I started working the water, but I really do not know what the hell it means.

We are putting the clams we get in the sacks that fifty pounds of onions come in. We count out one hundred and fifty to a sack and place them in the water in a creek that cuts into the marsh grass near the camp. Since they are still in the water, they will stay cool and be able to take a drink to refresh themselves, so the clams from the first day will still be fresh on the last day. And we have divided the creek into four sections, so each of us can keep track of his total clams for the trip.

When Carl and I each get two thousand clams from the mother lode hole, we stop working it. So we count them into sacks and take them to the creek that we call our Bank. And the total in my section already looks impressive and I feel good about that. Then Carl and I walk through the marsh grass to the camp and have sandwiches with four slices of bologna in each and potato chips and cool sodas. Then we fix sandwiches for Charlie and Jack and wrap them and get a big bag of chips for them and four sodas, then we run my skiff across the shallow bay to where they are working.

Now it is the middle of the afternoon. Carl and I are back on the outside of the narrow reef on the Portsmouth side, bullraking down off the reef in the waist deep water. The mother lode hole is farther out, and we are fairly close to the high shell banks that the pelicans like. The pelicans had been circling and diving for fish all morning. But now there isn't a pelican in sight and I wonder where they went. Normally they would start fussing when we get this close to their favorite places. And I wonder how a bird that is so truly beautiful and graceful as it flies and glides, can look so stumble bumbling when it dives for a fish. I mean the grace and style completely go. And they hit the water like a loose bag of sand, kersplash. Wings and legs all stumble. Then they bob up with the throat bag below their long bills all distended with a ton of water and maybe a fish. Someone said that they are successful only one out of every three

times. But I wonder how they can be successful even that one time. I mean after ten thousand years of practice, or however long, you would think that they would have their diving down to something really graceful by now. But the osprey really has his diving down to a magnificent science. Style and grace and efficiency all the way. They fly high enough over the water so their shadows do not show and so they can cover a large area. And when they see a fish close to the surface, they suddenly hover and hover until they are certain and have all the calculations of decent angle and decent speed calculated. Then they fold their wings and nose over and dive like the fastest arrow. Then they pull out right at the right split second, extend their claws, and hit the water just enough. The same someone said that they are also successful only one out of every three times. But osprey look a whole damn sight better doing it than pelicans. So I wonder again where the pelicans went.

There has not been even a breath of wind all day. And with this dead heat, the humidity has been almost unbearable. And the sun has looked a little funny like it is shining from behind thin gauze. So now and then Carl and I dunk ourselves completely into the water so for a few minutes afterwards the evaporation cools us some. Charlie and Jack are still much further out over in the shallow bay. And they are still hand clamming, so they are laid out up to their necks in the water so they are staying much cooler than Carl and I. So I think about switching to hand clamming so I can stay cooler. But I enjoy bullraking a lot more than hand clamming so I decide to stay with bullraking and continue to suffer. A bullrake looks like an overturned rectangular basket. It is about twenty inches long by twelve inches deep, made of iron rods spaced an inch apart so the sand and shells can wash out when it is dunked in the water. On one side of the basket opening is a flat bar for going along the bottom smoothly. The other side of the opening has a row of very sharp three inch long teeth. A seven foot long aluminum tee-handle is fastened to this overturned basket with clamps. So you pull the handle in short strong pulls along the bottoms and the teeth loosen shells and clams and sand and these fill the basket. Then you carefully turn the basket over and dunk it several times to wash it, then pick out the clams that you get. But the teeth do not want to stay in such hard bottom, so we have to keep forcing them to. So we have developed strong muscles in our hands and wrists and forearms. And just handling such a heavy tool all day requires a lot of stamina. So we have developed strong shoulder and back and leg muscles also. We have plastic tubs tied to a belt loop of our jeans with about three feet of thick string. So as we get clams, we put them in the tubs. Then when the tubs get full, we go to our skiffs and count the clams into the onion sacks. Carl makes his pulls with brute strength only. But I do not have Carl's strength, so I make my pulls smarter and with more finesse. But Carl's brute strength usually beats me on total clams for the day. But I don't mind, not really. But I keep trying to learn to pull smarter anyway.

I see the storm when it first begins to form itself down toward Core Sound. It isn't anything more than an area on the horizon where the light blue has begun to deepen a bit. A weekend boater wouldn't have noticed it. But after you have worked the water for awhile you learn the first signs. And when I look again in a few minutes, it has deepened more and soon it will begin to darken. So I think, 'thunderstorm building, that's why no wind, sun behind gauze, and pelicans gone.' But it has just begun to build, so there isn't any hurry. But I holler to Carl anyway and point and he looks and waves his hand that he understands. Carl is about forty yards on the other side of my skiff towards the mother lode hole. My skiff is staked off up fairly close to the narrow reef. And I am about thirty yards from it toward the high shell banks. Charlie and Jack are about a hundred and fifty yards from us over inside the shallow bay. And they are each about thirty yards from Charlie's skiff. But I don't holler to them because they couldn't hear me even if I holler as loud as I could. But they have been working the water for a long time and they know the signs, so they will see it soon. So I think, 'well a good thunderstorm will cool things off a lot, and that will be welcome, and you've been through a hundred thunderstorms, so this will be just one more.' So I forget about it for awhile. Because I am getting about twenty-five clams to a pull consistently and there isn't any thing shabby about that.

Beside we are way out here from Ocracoke, so there isn't anything that we can do but stay and weather it. Because if you run before every storm that comes along, especially in summer, you'll never get any work done and therefore not make any money. And we are already saltwater wet anyway, so rain is just freshwater wet and actually feels good as it washes off the saltwater. Besides thunderstorms are normally rather confined, and often will miss you entirely, or skirt by so you just get some of it. And the odds of getting struck by lightning are great, in spite of what Larry says and his charred meat Long Island friend also. So what I normally do is just go to my skiff and put on my foul weather coat because the first driving rain has a cold sting, and stay close to my skiff to make certain it doesn't get loose in the wind, and turn my back to the worst of it and stand there and weather whatever comes. If there is a lot of close lightning, I get up on a bank out of the water because lightening travels well in water. But the worst of a thunderstorm is in the leading edge. That is when the wind drives the rain sideways and the flashes and concussions are all around. Then it settles down to just a summer shower and you can go back to work if you want to, until the trailing edge passes when things worsen somewhat but not as much as during the leading edge.

When I look again I see Charlie and Jack come up from being laid out in the water like they were sprung. I mean suddenly they are upright and starting to run for Charlies's skiff like they are running in side by side tires that are in rows. But running in knee deep water pulling tubs full of clams is very awkward, so they are stumbling along more than they are running. So I look back over my shoulder and see that the whole sky to the southwest toward Cedar Island is an ugly dark blue that is quickly becoming black. I mean those ugly damn clouds are rolling and piling higher and higher like some gigantic bulldozer blade is behind them piling them up and up and over and over. And there is a solid wall of rain beneath them, and it is coming fast and is almost here. So I start to holler to Carl, but see that he sees it. So I start getting out of the waist deep water and to the narrow reef fast. And once in the ankle deep water beside the reef I start for my skiff, the bullrake in one hand and the other hand pulling the tub by the string, trying to get to my skiff before the first blast of the hard wind that I know is coming hits it. And I almost make it, but not quite. And when the first wind blast hits me and knocks me off stride and down on one knee, it also lifts the bow of my skiff clear of the water in one big jerk which stretches the bowline suddenly as tight as a drum which snatches the iron stake out of the bottom and flying like it had been stuck in jello and not in three feet of packed sand and shell. So now my skiff is loose and it shutters full length and it starts to buck wildly in the sudden swells that have arisen. And just as the backward momentum gets into my skiff that will send it racing across the five miles to Ocracokes southern shore in five minutes, the iron stake comes down and hits five or six feet in front of me. So right away I drop my bullrake and jump and dive for the stake, and when I do the tub jerks and spills the clams and now the wind has it too. But I have the stake. But now I am being pulled along too. But I get my feet out in front of me and they go into a slight depression in the bottom and dig in. So now I have something to brace against. So I have my feet braced in the depression and I have the stake in both hands where the bowline is tied. So I lean far back and brace my whole body against the sudden snatches and jolts of my skiff that the wind and the swells have put into it like it is a toy boat. But Jesus Christ himself cannot get my skiff loose from me now and I god damn mean that. Then I realize that the sideways rain is hitting my back and shoulders and head like a thousand cold knives and it hurts like hell, but I cannot do anything about that right now. So I look and see that Carl has dumped his clams and is using his tub as a shield against the sideways rain, and is slowly coming toward me doubled over by the wind. My skiff does another violent shutter dance, but still I will not be budged. So I look over my shoulder and see Charlie and Jack as vague figures in the wall of rain. They look like toy men running in a frantic dance of their own. Because Charlie's skiff is loose too. But it is gone from them. It is already fifty yards from them. It already has raced itself that far that fast in spite of their running and almost being to it when the first blast hit. But it has already beached itself on the inside of the narrow reef, so it cannot go any farther than that. But with the wind and the swells, it is beating the shit out of itself on the reef. But I cannot do anything to help it or them right now.

So my arms and legs begin to tremble from the too much strain too quickly. And my grip on the stake isn't the vice grip that it was several minutes ago. But since I must not weaken, I decide that I simply will not weaken. But I know that I am weakening in spite of that decision. So I look and see that Carl isn't very far away now and I know that I can hold on for that long. Then in a minute Carl has hold of the bowline too and right away the strain eases considerably. So for another minute we just hold on to the bowline and try to calm our breathing that is coming in ragged gasps. Then I try to say the wise crack, "are we having fun yet?" But it comes out too feeble in the loud wind for Carl to hear. Then after another minute our breathing is more regular so Carl asks me if I'm all right and I say yeah but my elbows feel pretty torn up from diving onto the shells going after the stake then getting dragged along through them. So he bends and looks and says that they look like mostly scrapes and no real bad cuts so I say good. Then after another minute I ask Carl if he can hold my skiff while I get our foul weather coats and he says yeah that the hard hitting rain is hurting like hell and I say yeah me too. So I approach my skiff carefully from the side because it is still doing its bouncing dance and untie the tub from my belt loop and put that in then reach into the seat compartment and get our foul weather coats and put mine on. Then I go give Carl his and he puts it on then unties his tub and I go put that in my skiff. Then I go get my bullrake up on the reef where I dropped it and go put that in. Then go get Carl's bullrake where he dropped it and go put that in. Now I am back and we are both holding the bowline, but my breathing is in ragged gasps again. So for a minute we just stand here with our backs to the worst of it. But with our thick foul weather coats on with the hoods up, the getting hit by a thousand cold knives eases a lot. So now there is just the sound of the wind rushing past and the sound of the rain hitting my coat and the sound of my hard breathing inside the hood.

So I say, "it should ease soon, the leading edge should be about by."

And Carl says, "I'm ready when it is."

And I say, "I'm with you," so we both laugh. But they are feeble laughs because we realize that even though the immediate crisis of my loose skiff has passed we are still a long way from being out of this mess.

Then I remember Charlie and Jack, so I look back over my shoulder and see that they finally got to Charlie's skiff and now they have it off the reef and out in the thigh deep water and Charlie is in it and starting the outboard while Jack is trying his best to hold the skiff in the wind and the rain and the swells.

So I say, "Charlie's skiff got on the reef, but they have it off now and they're trying to make a run for the camp."

And Carl says, "I forgot about them. Bet the camp is torn all to hell."

"Yeah, me too."

"Let's make a run for it too, Keith, this mess isn't easing."

"Okay, can you hold her?"

"Yeah."

So I go get beside my skiff and put both hands on the gunnel, and take a second to time my skiff's dance, then at the right time I throw my right leg up and over the gunnel like I am mounting a horse. And I am in it, so I go and throw off the tilt catch on the outboard and drop the lower unit into the water and knock it out of gear and turn the throttle to start and snatch the pullcord and it starts. All this in single movement. So I holler, "okay!" So now Carl is beside my skiff and he throws in the stake and bowline, then he has both hands on the gunnel and at the right time he throws his leg like he is mounting a horse, and he is in also.

Then the wind quickly has us spinning out well away from the reef, so I put the outboard in gear and give it some gas and right away my skiff starts rolling like hell as it goes along the swells rather than into them. So Carl unties the stake from the bowline and hands me the bowline and I pull it tight from the bow so we can stand and be steadied somewhat by it and be out of the bow spray pretty much. Then I see that there is already four or five inches of water in the bottom of my skiff so I bend and pull the self bailing plug that is in the stern so my skiff will bail itself as we run. Then I holler to Carl against the wind, "I'm going to run along these swells until we get beyond Shell Castle to the southeast, then turn into the wind until we are beyond it to the southwest, then come back to Shell Castle with the wind!" And Carl hollers okay.

But the wind blows us east towards Portsmouth village and the Inlet by about the same distance that we traveled to get beyond Shell Castle. But we knew it would so this is okay. Then I decide that it is time to make the turn into the wind so I say, "I'll make the turn on three, Carl," and he says okay and he spreads his legs further and steadies himself more because the bow won't want to go into the wind and it has to be timed precisely. So as we run along the side of a swell and start up it I say, "one, two, three," and at three we are at the crest of the swell, so I slam the steering arm hard left so the bow will go hard right as the bow starts down into the swell trough. The bow does and we are into the wind but spray comes off the bow in solid sheets but we stay into the wind.

So now it is just a matter of slowly beating our way southwest to beyond Shell Castle. And our legs quickly adjust to absorbing the shock of going over and into the endless fast coming swells. But Carl can stand with his back to the worst of it. But I have to stand sideways to it so I can see where we are going as I look from beneath my hood. But the wind driven rain and the salt spray hit my face anyway. But there isn't anything I can do about it. So my eyes sting and I can taste saltwater so I keep spitting and I realize that I am cold.

So I lean toward Carl and holler against the wind, "that first blast had to be fifty to sixty, Carl!"

"At least, and it hasn't eased yet."

"It damn near sent my skinny ass flying."

"That's what you get for not having an ass. Next time tie a cinderblock to it."

"Thanks alot, smart ass," and we both laugh.

Then I say, "Carl there isn't any lightening."

"And I haven't missed it one bit."

"But if there isn't any lightning, then this mess isn't a thunderstorm."

"It's close enough so I can't tell the difference," Carl says.

But I wonder about there not being any lightning anyway. And I wish I could wipe my eyes and I wish I had a cigarette and I wish I had on the flannel shirt that is in the seat compartment because now I am shivering and the taste of the saltwater is terrible so I keep spitting. But finally we are far enough beyond, so I holler, "Carl we're far enough beyond now, I'll turn on three," and he hollers okay. So on three I slam the steering arm hard left and the bow goes hard right and now we are flying with the swells and the wind toward Shell Castle. So Carl hollers, "hold her, Newt, she's heading for the barn!" And we both hoot and holler like wild racing cowboys because now this is a real fun ride.

But we approach Shell Castle too quickly with the wind. I look but I don't see the tents. "The tents are down, Carl!" But he is looking also so he already knows that. Then I see Charlie walking from the camp to the Bank Creek. Now we round the west side of Shell Castle too quickly. I see Jack taking sacked clams from Charlie's anchored off skiff to their sections of the creek. The Bank creek is in the lee of the wind and therefore is a safe small harbor. So I kill the outboard and put it on tilt and put in the self bailing plug. But we are still nearing too quickly. So I go stand beside Carl in the bow. He has the bowline and at the right time he jumps into the waist deep water. Then in the next second I jump into the knee deep water, holding the gunnel close to the bow. Carl holds the bowline as it comes tight while I cushion the jolt. Then my skiff quickly settles down and stops here in the fairly calm water at the mouth of the Bank creek.

Then Charlie comes through the marsh grass and says, "fellas, the camp is torn all to hell and gone." But we aren't surprised so we don't say anything. Then Charlie says, "we were getting worried about y'all."

"It took forever to beat around the south side," Carl says.

And I say, "Charlie, is your skiff hurt from the beating?"

"Doesn't seem to be," he says. But I am skeptical because it did beat the shit out of itself on the reef.

So Carl and I get my skiff staked off at the bow and anchored off at the stern. Then we put our sacked clams in our sections of the creek. Now we are just standing around here in the still sideways rain with the wind not really too bad where we are. We all look a little wild eyed and a little dazed from all this too much too soon mess. But we are here now and safe. So it is simply a matter of putting the camp back together as best we can, then going on from there.

And the camp is torn all to hell and gone. And it looks like a big hand had come along and given it a hard swipe. And our tents were flattened by that swipe. But righting mine and Carl's is simply a matter of getting it upright again, then redriving the stakes. But the center pole of Charlie and Jack's is snapped. So we go look among the debris of old high water marks for something to scab with. And Jack finds a narrow flat board that is till sturdy so we scab that to the snapped pole with string and hope that it will hold. Then we gather everything that had been knocked over or tumbled or blown into the marsh grass, and reorganize it as best we can. But the cook stove and the lantern are soaked and we can't get them to stay lit in the wind. So finally we give up on them and say to hell with them and everything else too until morning and go get into our tents. Because dark has come long before it should. Because it just goes from can see to can't see in what seems like a very few minutes. And Carl and I are blue and shivering and our water puckered hands and feet are white shriveled. But with dry clothes we begin to get warm then flushed then drowsy. But with warm comes the pain of my elbow and forearm scrapes, so I mercurochrome them as best I can. Then I have a peanut butter and jelly sandwich. Then a can of sardines with crackers. And I finish with cookies. I am also finishing my third beer, and the beer tastes the best of everything. Carl and I are sitting cross-legged in the tent with an on flashlight between us. The wind seems to have eased somewhat, but not by much. Because the tent is flapping and popping and the still sideways rain is pelting it like a thousand thrown pebbles.

"It's still blowing forty to fifty, Carl."

"Yeah, this has turned into a real blow all right."

"What do you think?"

"I don't know. All we can do is wait until morning. Maybe it will blow itself out."

"Sure hope so. We're off to a good start with clams, and I'd hate for the trip to get busted."

"Yeah, well we'll see how things look in the morning."

"I feel like I've been drug through a keyhole backwards."

And Carl laughs. "We won't have any trouble getting to sleep tonight that's for sure."

"You ready?" And Carl nods and I off the flashlight and we start getting comfortable further in our sleeping bags. Then Jack and Charlie let out a loud string of cuss words. And Carl asks what's wrong and they answer that their center pole snapped again. So I on the flashlight and Carl and I look at each other hopelessly, and we can hear them struggling around like caged animals in their fallen tent. So I say, "y'all may as well come get in our tent. We'll worry about it in the morning."

With the waterproof floor to our tent, and by being very careful, we have managed to keep things fairly dry. But now with the awkward confusion of Jack and Charlie getting into our tent that wasn't made for four, the wet is getting everywhere. But finally we get situated and begin to settle down. I am lying on my back all scrunched against the tent side. I can feel the flap and the pop of the wind and the pelt of the rain, but I am too exhausted to let it bother me for long. I have my arms crossed on my chest because my elbow and forearms hurt when they touch anything. And I am thinking that the best thing about being a bay fisherman in an open skiff is the complete freedom of it. But the worse thing is not having anywhere to go when it gets bad. The trawler guys can get inside the wheelhouse out of it when they aren't working the sterndeck. They can get in out of it for awhile anyway. But whatever the season, whatever the weather, the skiff fisherman has to suffer directly whatever comes without relief. And there isn't anything any more dreary than having to work on in the rain, and can't get out of it for awhile anyway. And what has the water terrible as hell for a skiff, isn't necessarily all that bad for a trawler. It is all relative to boat size. Because three foot swells spell literal danger in a skiff, while a trawler hardly notices three foot swells. But Oscar was right, around Swansboro we have plenty of places to run to get away from the bad. But up here we are dead out in it whatever comes and this mess too. But thankfully we have this tent between us and it now. And as bad as that first blast was and right after it, it really wasn't that bad. Because once you have worked on the water for awhile you get use to misery and discomfort because that just comes with the job. And as bad as things are, they always can get worse. You have certainly learned that. Then when things get worse, you simply adjust to that, because things could get still worse. And the very worse that could happen now would be for Shell Castle to get over washed by a huge storm serge wave. But they come with hurricanes and whatever it is this mess isn't a hurricane. And storm serges require many miles of deep water in which to build and gain momentum. But we don't have those conditions up here around Shell Castle. So the southwest side will just suffer a lot of erosion from the continuous swell punishment but that's about all. So what is ahead for us is more wind and more rain and the dreary misery that comes with them. So the worse that can happen tonight would be for our tent to fall too. And if it does, I'm god damn not going to worry about it, because my elbows and forearms hurt like hell and I'm completely knocked out from exhaustion.

I wake in the black dark when Jack hollers that his feet are getting wet. Carl ons the flashlight then kneels at the tent flap and gets the flap outside and tied down so it can't come loose again. Jack keeps muttering cuss words about his newly wet feet. Charlie asks what time it is. I look at the clock in the plastic bag and say two ten then I reach for a cigarette. Then I say that it seems to have eased. Because I am still scrunched against the tent side but don't feel the flap and pop and pelt any longer.

"Oh shit, it's backing around!" I holler. Because we pitched the tent facing Portsmouth village. And that is east. This mess first came from the southwest. Now it is coming from the east. The flap and pop and pelt is on the front. So this mess has backed counter clockwise from southwest to east. And it will continue backing until it gets northeast by dawn. Because this mess is a northeaster!

"This mess is a northeaster!," I say.

"No way," Charlie says, "two early for them. Don't have them until fall."

"September is just two weeks away," Carl says.

"So that's what this is, a god damn northeaster," I say like someone has just given me a present.

"Well, we still can't do anything about it," Charlie says.

"But I feel better knowing," I say.

"My feet are soaked, just look at them," Jacks says.

"Maybe it will blow itself out by morning," Carl says.

But we know it won't, at least not by morning," Carl says. So I lie here and think, a northeaster, just a northeaster. Hell, I've been through a hundred northeasters. And I feel better now that I know what this mess is. But I was really worried when I didn't know what it was. Because it is the unknown that we fear the most. But the discomfort of getting through a northeaster won't be any easier, now that we know. But knowing, we can better deal with it because we have been through them before. But Oscar said to run like hell because it's going to be bad and it's going to stay awhile, when it starts to back around. But it's too late for running now because we are up here and not down there, and it's already been bad so all that's ahead is just more of the same. So I put out the cigarette and I off the flashlight and I get my arms back across my chest so my elbows and forearms won't hurt so much.

CHAPTER ELEVEN

Yeah, at dawn she is puffing along forty to fifty from the northeast all right. And with sideways rain still. Then the can't see becomes can see in a very few minutes. And the first thing for us to do is check the skiffs. So we go to the Bank creek and we see that there is a foot of rainwater in each skiff. But it would take twice that or more before they even come close to sinking but we go ahead and bail them anyway. And the skiffs have ridden the night well because the Bank creek is in the lee for east and now northeast winds also, so it is still a safe harbor and we are glad about that. But wading out waist deep into the now cold water after the deliciously nice warm and dry takes grim determination but that is just a part of the job too.

And it takes awhile but we finally get mine and Carl's tent loosed then turned and fastened down again facing southwest, then get Charlie's tent rigged like a porch awning coming from our tent. Then Charlie and Jack take awhile but they finally get the cook stove dried out and properly sheltered from the wind. Then they have coffee happily perking away and the coffee smells better than sex feels. Because we can endure anything, just give us our coffee first. And we have on flannel shirts and sweaters under our foul weather coats, and with our hoods up and walking stiffly and bulkily around the camp, we look like a small gathering of eighty year old monks stirring about in the dreary morning light. But the bacon and eggs and bread are a little damp. But there is plenty more hot coffee. And the juice of the canned peaches is like nectar because our throats are hoarse and sore from all of yesterday's hollering against the wind.

Then when everything is cleaned and put away, I go get into the tent to take a nap. Because there isn't a damn thing that we can do now but wait and see if it will soon blow itself out. But we know it won't, because northeasters normally take days to blow themselves out. But we are already here, and we don't want this trip busted yet, because we have really only just gotten started. So we talk cheerfully and hopefully during breakfast, but probably it is only wishful thinking.

I wake when Jack says, "yeah, it's the Coast Guard," as he gets back under the awning.

"That's what I figured, sounds like their launch," Carl says sitting on a cooler beside the front flap.

"What's wrong?" Charlie asks, coming awake in his sleeping bag next to mine.

"Coast Guard came to check on us," Jack answers, "I waved so they would know we're okay, they waved back."

Then I can hear the way off muffled drone of their launch as they finish their slow circle of Shell Castle, before starting back to Ocracoke. So I say, "that's damn nice of them."

"Yeah, they stay in when it's calm, then come out when no one else will. They're salty sons of bitches, that's for sure." Carl says.

So I say, "some of them are fourth and fifth generation Outer Bankers. Life saving is all they've done back to when they launched boats into the surf then rowed out to sinking ships off shore."

"They're saltier than I am," Charlie says as he gets out of his sleeping bag and goes out through the flap under the awning. "I'm tough, but not that tough."

So I remember what Ben Dixon Mac Neil said about them in The Hatterasman,' nowhere on the earth are there men who know the sea so profoundly, who know it and fear it and love it.' And I think, yeah, they're salty sons of bitches all right.

"Their launch is the new rollover kind," Jack says, "if it rolls bottom up, it will automatically right itself."

"How would you like to have been in the crew that had to keep rolling it until they were sure the bugs were worked out?" Carl asks.

"Not me, no damn way," Charlie answers.

"That launch would make a fine clam boat," Jack says.

"You'd have to get a whole hell of a lot of clams to pay for a quarter million dollar boat," Carl says.

"You reckon it costs that much," Jack asks.

"Damn near, probably," Carl answers.

So I get out of my sleeping bag and go out through the flap. And we go on small talking this way for awhile, sitting on coolers under the awning and trying to stay out of the wind and rain, because what else do we have to do? Then I push up my sleeves and hold my elbows so Carl can mercurochrome my still hurting scrapes real good. Then they start pushing up their sleeves and their pants legs and mercurochroming their here and there cuts and scrapes. So for awhile we have a mercurochrome party.

Then Charlie asks Carl if he has taken the fiberglass repair course out at the technical college. And Carl says no, but that he is seriously thinking about taking it because the yacht plant at Harkers Island is always looking for skilled fiberglass men and they pay damn good. And Charlie agrees and says let's take the course together the next time it's offered and Carl says okay. Then Jack says that he has been thinking about going back on the bread truck. That he guesses it really isn't too bad a job after all, and that if he really worked at building the route he could probably take home four hundred a week. And we agree that four hundred steady isn't bad money at all. So here we are again talking around the coming death of our clam fishery, without talking directly at it. Again making vague plans that maybe some day will be turned into concrete actions. Deciding to absolutely face the inevitable some time next year maybe. So I know again that it really does take all types of fishermen to make up a fishery. Larry, who is a good fisherman until beer and distorted fears distract him. Jack and Charlie, who drift to and from fishing and regular jobs by whim and mood without really planting their feet in either world. Carl, who is firmly committed to fishing, but who only wants to be a specialist in a world that is increasingly becoming diverse. Me, committed certainly, but having champagne taste and beer money and prone to hedge. So yeah, it really does take all types. So you can have one fisherman an ex-professor of philosophy, and the next a practicing illiterate. One a common thief, and the next a holy roller. Yeah, and everything in between. And all of us having decided to face the inevitable some time next year maybe.

But by now we have gotten antsy as hell with this just sitting around talking small talk and trying to stay out of the wind and rain. And the stubble beard itching is worse. And the unclean feeling of dried saltwater all over us is unpleasant. And how nice it would be just to brush our teeth. And an increasing odorous aroma is coming from inside our clothing whenever we move about. So Carl asks what time it is, and I pull back the flap and look in at the clock and say almost twelve. Then we go back to just sitting around and looking thoroughly bored and uncomfortable at each other. So I go ahead and ask the question outloud, "well fellas, what are we going to do,?" Because we have already enjoyed about as much of this misery as we can stand.

Then in a rush Jack says, "I would love a shower and clean dry clothes."

And Charlie says, 'I would love a cold beer and a thick hamburger."

And Carl says, "I would love a sit down shit instead of a squat in the marsh grass."

"So we go?" I say, because I would love all those things also.

"Well, let's just go to Ocracoke and get motel rooms for the night," Charlie says.

"Let's go the hell back to Swansboro, this trip's busted," Jack says.

"No, let's give it until in the morning, Jack, it could clear," Charlie says.

"You know it won't," Jack answers.

"But it could. Besides, we can see what's shaking with the girls on Ocracoke tonight," Charlie says.

"Hey, hadn't though of that," and Jack suddenly brightens.

"What about you, Carl?" I ask.

"Giving it until in the morning is fine with me. We're off to too good a start to give up before we have to."

"Hell, you and Keith are off to a good start. Keith especially, the lucky asshole," Jack says.

"Okay, so we go," I say ignoring Jack, "it's blowing as bad as it's going to, so the camp will be okay like it is."

"Let's all go in my skiff," Charlie says, "my fifty will get us there a lot faster than your thirty five horse, even with the four of us in it."

"No, I'm not leaving my skiff," I say.

"Hell, it'll be okay, it won't go anywhere," Charlie says.

"No, my skiff goes where I go."

"Suit yourself," Charlie shrugs, "let's go Jack."

"Better follow the crab pot floats, the tide's still down some," I say as we start gathering the things we will take with us.

Charlie and Jack are in a big hurry to get to Ocracoke. Now they are way ahead of Carl and I, and I begin to lose them in the sideways rain. Charlie is trying to get his skiff planed off, but all he is doing is bouncing from one swell to the next and throwing high sheets of spray each time they hit so hard, but still he doesn't back off the throttle. Carl and I, though, are slowly beating our way one swell at the time against the wind and the swells the way we did yesterday afternoon. We are standing and we have the bowline again pulled tight from the bow to steady us. Carl has his back to the worst of it, and I have my head down and am looking ahead from under my hood and am trying to avoid as much of it as possible, but my eyes are already saltwater stinging anyway. Once Shell Castle is out of sight astern, which isn't long, I no longer know our direction and have to navigate by reckoning. But that is fairly simple because the wind is blowing from the northeast and Ocracoke is a little north of that, so if I keep heading a little north of northeast we will get there eventually. But if I head a shade too much north, then we will miss Ocracoke on the right and head out into thirty miles of open Pamlico Sound. So we continue to slowly beat our way as I follow the crab pot floats and watch for shoals and gauge wind direction as best I can. Then ahead I see Charlie and Jack dead in the water and getting blown around and around by the wind and swells. Charlie is leaning far over the stern and he has his hands quickly working down at his outboard's prop. "They hit a crab pot line and they're dead in the water!" I holler and Carl nods. Then, "now they're loose and going again!" I holler and Carl nods.

Meanwhile we gain quite a bit on them. But now Charlie is jumping the tops of swells again, so we start losing them. But he doesn't go fifty yards and they're dead in the water again and he is leaning far over the stern. So I holler, "they just hit another one!", and Carl shakes his head. And I holler, "I told them to follow the crab pots, not to run over every god damn one they find!" And Carl says, "what did you expect from those two idiots?!" And I say, "well, at least they've been getting along." And Carl says, "they've had too much else to think about, give them a chance." So we laugh.

Now I don't know where the hell Charlie and Jack are. But I don't care. Because ahead is the entrance to Ocracoke harbor, right where I knew it would be. So I think, 'are you a navigator, or what!' and I holler, "we're here, harbor's dead ahead, am I a navigator or what!" And Carl hollers, "you're some fine navigator all right!" And I gloat, "damn straight I am!" And we laugh because we are glad as hell to be here because beating it against the wind and swells never is a fun run. "There's Charlie and Jack coming up astern!" Carl hollers. And I look, "when did we pass them, I didn't see them?" And Carl shrugs, "they probably missed a crab pot and doubled back to hit it so they wouldn't miss one between Shell Castle and Ocracoke!" So we laugh.

Then as soon as we are inside the breakwater boulders the wind falls to nothing and the water flattens out. And the rain is falling straight down. And it is like suddenly going from a nightmare to a very pleasant dream. But Carl and I still have that wild eyed stunned look from the just passed too much too soon danger. But we are safely here finally, and we are happy as hell about that.

Then I see a Guardsman standing on the porch of the Station looking at us through binoculars, so I give him a thumbs up as we pass and he waves.

So Carl and I are contented like two pigs in heavy duty slop now. He sprawled out and leaning against a pillow on his big double bed, me sprawled out and leaning back against a pillow on my big double bed, here in our motel room just down the road from the dock. And we are warm and dry and shaved and showered and sit down shifted, and full as hell from the hamburger steak and fries and salad and tea at the restaurant next door. And we each have an iced beer on the nightstand, and a cigarette burning in the ashtray. Yeah, contented like two pigs in heavy duty slop all right. But the forecast on the television on the dresser across the room is for this mess to continue. So this trip is busted all to hell and we hate the hell out of that. And we could kick our asses for not knocking down the camp and bringing everything with us so we wouldn't have to run back to Shell Castle tomorrow to get it. But that is spilt milk, and we cannot do anything about that. Nothing to do now but tomorrow just grit our teeth and do it.

And it is a welcome relief being away from Jack and Charlie for the first time in two days. Because they left awhile ago to go to a bar they heard about just outside Ocracoke village on the road to the Cape Hatteras ferry landing. But they started arguing as soon as they got in their room next door to ours. Because Carl and I could hear Jack right away start into Charlie about his no couthness when around girls and never mind about the color of their panties anyway. And so on and so forth, and back and forth like that for awhile. But they are gone and it is quiet now with a game show on low on the television across the room. But I can still hear the wind rush in my ears and feel the rain pelt and feel my skiff's endless rolling and pitching and slamming. And my eyes are bloodshot and they still sting from the saltwater spray, and they feel like they have sand in them.

"I'm going down to the dock and see if that fella has eyewash in his store," I say, "want to go?"

"It's too comfortable here," Carl answers, "and I need to call Sara, I'm sure she's worried."

So I pay for the eyewash, but I don't leave. The older fisherman is still sitting one cheeked on the stool behind the counter with his left leg outstretched resting. "Mind if we talk some?" I ask. And he looks at me and shakes his head no he doesn't mind. But I know that Ocracokers only tolerate strangers for the tourist dollars. But they don't appreciate direct questioning very much, never have, never will. But I go ahead, anyway. Because there are several things I simply have to know. And maybe from an older fisherman to a younger fisherman, he will tell me. "What's a sun dog?"

And he just looks at me for a long minute, then finally says, "could point one out better than tell you."

"Could you give me an idea? What to look for? Maybe I can save myself a lot of punishment next time."

"Well, you don't deny the sea. You go ahead and face her, whatever she brings." He says as he decides outloud whether to answer and how much to say. "They're small suns inside a circle around the sun. They follow it like a dog does a man. You'll never notice them if you don't know what to look for. Mean a sudden change in the weather is coming.   More than likely a real bad change. So you may as well stay tied to the dock."

"I didn't know."

"Well, if you don't know, you just don't know. Can't be faulted too much for that. But once a sign's been pointed out to you, you'll know. Then it's up to you whether you heed it. Some do, some don't, depends."

"Are there many signs like sun dogs?"

"Only a few that really count. Takes time to learn to read them though. And being up here, and having someone to point them out to you. Most won't point them out, some will, depends."

So I nod that I understand that Ocracokers don't easily warm to strangers. But now I know that if I spend time up here, and if I don't deny the sea, and if I don't make a habit of this, he will point things out to me.   Then I say, "where did this blow come from anyway, there wasn't anything about it on the forecasts?"

"Pamlico Sound's big enough to generate it's own weather. And having the Gulf Stream just offshore don't help none."

So I nod that I understand that. So that is why Oscar

Schneider said not to pay too much attention to forecasts when up here. "One more question, then I won't bother you anymore," I say and he nods. But I can tell that he has probably talked more in the last few minutes than he has talked all week, and it is getting tiresome to him. "Could a fella make a living up here with a twenty five footer rigged one man?"

"Some still do, some don't, depends."

"I'm thinking about moving up here and bringing one."

"Cedar Island would be better. Counting on these ferrys to get your catch to market is expensive and time consuming."

"But could I compete with the big trawlers?"

"Wouldn't want to. There's a world of sloughs between here and Cedar Island for a shallow draft boat. Mainly work flounder, though, they always sell good. Get yourself some Raleigh restaurants for steady customers, and you've cut out the middleman."

"I really appreciate your talking with me," I say and he nods. And inside I am really excited about how much I have learned.

"You didn't bring in your gear," he says.

"No sir, left it on Shell Castle. Thought this mess would blow itself out."

"If you don't know, you just don't know," he smiles, "but think how good you'll feel when you do know."

"I'm Keith Englund," and I put out my hand.

"Luther Styron," and we shake, and I can feel his tough flat old fisherman's hand.

"How'd you hurt your leg?"

"A deck winch caught me awhile back."

"Hope it gets better."

"It's about as good as it's going to get, but I manage."

So I thank him and say I appreciate it again, and I try very hard to not sound too gushy. Because damn am I excited!

Somehow I find the ringing telephone in the dark. When I say hello, a man says he's a Deputy Sheriff, and that they are holding Jack and Charlie down at the Magistrate's office. When I ask what the charges are, he says drunk and disorderly and fighting and property damage for starters, and that he and the Magistrate are still deciding about resisting arrest. But that either way, a hundred a piece will bail them out if I want to, or not, it doesn't matter to him. But I say, no, that I'll come get them. Then I ask what happened. And he says the best he can figure out one of them said something to one of the local girls, which set off the local fellas. Then both of them put their backs to a wall and took on all comers, and made a right fair showing for themselves for awhile. But were right smart banged up for their efforts now. So I say okay I'll be down in a few minutes. Then I ask where the Magistrate's office is and he tells me and I thank him and we hang up.

Meanwhile Carl had oned the desklamp when the conversation began, and I can tell by his grim mouth that he is sure enough pissed. "Those idiots!?" Carl says as soon as I hang up. And I say, yeah, then tell him everything.

"Jesus H. Christ, that's what we get for associating with

idiots!" Carl says. Then he says, "go back to sleep, I'll go, no need in both of us losing sleep." Then Carl says he has a hundred if I have a hundred, and I say yeah in my wallet on the dresser. Then Carl says, "Jesus H. Christ, save us from the idiots of this world!" Because Carl is definitely pissed.

Then later I wake when Carl gets in bed muttering to himself. Then through the wall I hear Jack start into Charlie, "look what you've gone and done! Just look! Look at my eye. Didn't I tell you that you ain't fit to be around people? Here I get my eye blacked and my head whipped on, then get thrown in jail all because of your no count ass. Now Carl is pissed at us. And Keith, probably is too. When we get back to Swansboro I'm going to build a cage and keep your sorry ass in it. You ain't got no couth, Charlie!" Then Charlie starts with his, "buts," but I've heard it all before, and it won't change anything, so I go back to sleep.

CHAPTER TWELVE

So here we go again. But this time when we pass the breakwater boulders at the harbor entrance, we hang a left and run close in to Ocracoke's lee shore on our way toward Teach's Hole and the Inlet. The wind has eased to thirty to forty and the rain isn't pelting quite as hard, but it is still a truly miserable morning for a boat ride. And Charlie and Jack look as banged up as we expected them to, but at breakfast at the Restuarant, Carl and I don't mention either the fight or jail or their wounds and they seem relieved. Once, though, I couldn't help smiling at Carl over how very gently they ate with their split lips and loose teeth and bruised jaws. And I thought 'suffer, assholes, suffer'.

So the plan is for us to hang a right just past Teach's Hole and before the Inlet for the long run southwest with the wind the way Carl and I had done Tuesday afternoon when this mess first started. But this run will be about three times the distance of that run. But running with the wind instead of against the wind will be a lot easier and quicker. Besides, with low tide in an hour or so, a straight shot south from the harbor entrance to Shell Castle would be almost impossible because we would continually run aground on the shoals. So this is really our only choice. And by heading more west than southwest we can make use of the deep water of Wallace Channel pretty well all the way, until close to Shell Castle where it will get fairly shoaly during low tide. And I had made reservations for us on the last ferry back to Cedar Island late this afternoon. So we have all day to get to Shell Castle, knock down the camp, load everything, then the straight shot back to Ocracoke in the middle of the afternoon when the tide is up. So that is the plan.

But let me put this in perspective. Here we are in seventeen foot open skiffs, about to spend all day out in a screaming northeaster that is still howling along none to shabbily, with the running swells whitecapped and foamy, and the steady rain still so thick that we can't see more than a hundred yards in any direction. And if, if, we keep the wind to our back and head a little west of that, we should, should, make Shell Castle without a problem. But if we head just a shade too far southwest, then what would be ahead of us would be thirty or more miles of the huge Pamlico Sound and more serious trouble than I care to think about. Because remember that we can't see more than a hundred yards in any direction. And Shell Castle is really quite small out there in the middle of all this whole hell of a lot of open unruly water. So Wormshoe was correct in his prediction, you couldn't drive a sixteen penny nail up our asses with a ten pound sledgehammer.

And Charlie and Jack are running about thirty yards ahead of Carl and I. And Charlie is wisely keeping his speed moderate, so maybe his is capable of learning from past mistakes after all. And just past Teach's Hole and before the Inlet, Charlie looks back at me. I have the chart visualized in my mind, and I have been deciding when to hang the right with the wind. And now I decide that now is about as good a time as any. So I throw out my right arm and Charlie hangs the right. Then when we get to where he hung the right, we hang a right, and there they are ahead and we are still in tandem. But real fast we are away from the lee of the shore, and out in the howling wind and the foamy swells. But when you have a sturdy skiff and a strong outboard, and when you have worked the water in storms long enough to know what you're doing, then running with the wind in a screaming northeaster can be a real blast. I mean all of a sudden Carl and I start to really enjoy ourselves again. We are standing braced and have the bowline pulled tight so we are steady, and we are fast running over and into and over and into the whitecapped swells like they are a fun endless roller coaster. So Carl hollers, "hold her Newt, she's heading for the barn!" again. Then we both hoot and holler like wild racing cowboys, again. But soon we get quiet, because this run is going to be long as hell and the monotony of the endless passing swells quickly sets in.

But I get quiet before Carl does because I remember that it is my job to concentrate on navigation. Because we can hoot and holler and have a good time on another trip. But now, first we must find Shell Castle that hopefully is up ahead somewhere and easily findable. So I have the chart visualized again, and I have our progress pinpointed on it as we make it, and I know that we must be well into Wallace Channel by now. But something tells me that we need to veer more westerly now. So when Charlie looks back again, instead of motioning him straight ahead, I motion him a shade to the right, and he makes that correction, and we continue on the roller coaster. Because they look to me to navigate, now that navigation is required. Because it is my skiff, so I am the Captain, where if we were in Carl's skiff he would be the Captain. But we have been in my skiff all the times we have come up here, so from necessity and from desire I am more familiar with these waters. Just the way the car driver always watches the road and the turns, while the passenger does the sight seeing. And this is Charlie and Jack's first trip up here so they don't know these waters at all, and hopefully Charlie won't decide to haul ass off out into the unknown the way he did yesterday.

So we are far enough into Wallace Channel by now to be about where the sailing vessels use to make their turnbacks to get into Portsmouth harbor two hundred and eighty some years ago when Portsmouth was the biggest city from Virginia to Florida. Until they fell the trees and their cattle ate the grasses, so the wind simply picked up the island sand and tossed it in the harbor to harshly demonstrate the simple lesson of don't screw around with mother nature. Until they then had to walk a mile or more across the shallows just to get to Portsmouth village where the wharves and the warehouses then stood idle and useless. Until they then built the wharves and warehouses on Shell Castle. Until finally the mainland ports grew sufficiently to where the sharp trading merchants up here were no longer needed. Until Portsmouth finally strangled itself to death, and everyone but them said good riddance. But stop the reminiscing now, concentrate on the navigation now, because first we must find Shell Castle that is up ahead somewhere. Then something tells me that we need to veer more westerly still. But I am not certain, so I visualize the chart harder and our progress on it, and try to decide.

But before I can decide, I see Charlie suddenly cut throttle entirely and throw his outboard out of gear all in one motion, and point and holler to Jack about something in the water dead ahead and a little right. So I cut throttle also, and at that instant Charlie's skiff raises itself and his outboard's lower unit kicks back, and I start to holler, 'Carl, they've hit a shoal!', but all I get out is the "Carl," part when I see the right side of Charlies's stern come completely away from the hull. I mean suddenly there is a god damn two foot gap on the right side! And as Charlie starts to look down and back to see the damage, he does a backflip like an unseen hand had him and he is thrown over the stern and out of his skiff and into the water. And I hear Carl holler, "Jesus H. Christ!", and I see Jack tumble into the bow head first. And I see that Charlie's skiff is beyond the shoal now and it begins to shiver and roll drunkenly in the swells. Then I see Charlie pop up in the water ahead, all wild eyed and spitting water and looking all around like he doesn't know where he is or how the hell he got there. Then Carl has a coil of spare line out of a seat compartment, and I begin to ease us closer and closer to Charlie. But without much power I don't have steerage, and the wind and swells from astern begin to push my skiff ahead by lurches. And suddenly I know that we will run over

Charlie. Then as we go into the trough of a swell, the stern of my skiff comes around, so now we are broadside to it and Carl and I lose our footing and I grab the right side gunnel to keep from going overboard and Carl falls to his knees in the bottom of my skiff and grabs the left side gunnel with both hands. But we are closing with Charlie too fast and we are going to run over him, so I knock my outboard into reverse and give it throttle but there just isn't time enough for it to catch so there isn't anything I can do about running over Charlie. So Carl turns loose of the coil of spare line and gets on his knees at the left side gunnel and leans over and as far out as he can to try and grab Charlie before we hit him. But Charlie sees that we are going to run over him, so at the right time he suddenly submerges himself by pulling up his hands from deep in the water, just before my skiff is where he was. Meanwhile I cut throttle and knock my outboard out of gear in one motion and get on my knees at the right side gunnel and lean far out. And when Charlie comes up below me I grab his shirt and he grabs my arms and I holler, "I got him, Carl!" but Carl is already on his knees beside me. So we each take an arm and we stand crouched and we pull half drowned Charlies's wet ass into my skiff.

Then I quickly get back at my outboard. And I'm standing in a braced crouch and I'm looking all around trying to find where the hell Jack is and is he still afloat? Then a swell runs under us and raises us and I see Jack still afloat about twenty yards away and off to the side. But my skiff is rolling and pitching so badly that I am about to get knocked down again, so I give it some throttle and start running along the swells and now I have steerage again. And I head for Jack's downwind side so when we close with him we won't hit Charlie's skiff like we ran over Charlie. So I lean down and put my mouth to Carl's ear and holler against the wind, "should we tow from the bow, or from a stern cleat?" And Carl turns loose of Charlie and just lets him spit and sputter on his own lying there in the bottom of my skiff, and gets to a braced crouch holding the gunnel and looks. "Bow probably would be better, Keith, if we tow from a stern cleat we may swamp her whenever the line jerks." So I nod and say okay. Then Carl puts his mouth to my ear again and says, "let's put Charlie back in his skiff, then the two of them can move forward or back whatever it takes to keep the stern out of the water." So I nod and say okay again. Then Carl leans down and hollers into Charlie's ear what we are going to do , and Charlie nods and says okay and goes back to spitting and sputtering. So I look and see Charlie's skiff slowly spinning and rolling and pitching like a wounded run away top. Jack is a fairly hefty fella, so his weight all in the bow has the bow way down and the stern out of the water. And there that god damn two foot gap is on the right side! But it hasn't gotten any worse and the left side is holding, and that is damn good. And Jack is holding on for dear life with one hand, and bailing so fast the scoop looks like a blur. And as bad as things are, things can get a whole hell of a lot worse real fast if we aren't damn careful.

Then Carl cushions the shock of our skiffs coming together. Then he leans down and begins to tie one end of the coil of spare line to the bow eye of Charlie's skiff. Meanwhile Charlie puts both hands on his gunnel and jumps over into his skiff behind Jack. So I look at Jack standing there all white faced and scared eyed and I holler. "Did you shit in your pants when the stern pulled loose?" And Jack's mouth starts working open, close, open, close, like Wormshoe's does, and finally the words start coming out. "You god damn right! I didn't know what the hell happened. All of a sudden I was on my head in the bow. Wait till I get Charlie back to Swansboro. I'm going to kill him." So I laugh. But I think, 'this couldn't happen to two finer fellas.' But Carl and I are caught right in the middle of it too, so there's damn little satisfaction in it.

So Carl feeds out the line until it comes taunt, then we are underway towing Charlie and Jack, so I give the outboard more throttle. But they are going to have to do one hell of a balancing act there in the bow to keep water from rushing in the open gapped stern and sinking them in seconds. But dead in the water without steerage the way they are, the astern wind keeps trying to blow them around and to the side of Carl and I, so I give the outboard even more throttle. But then my skiff starts nosing into swells and throwing bad spray, but there isn't anything I can do about that. So I holler to Carl, "where the hell are we?!" and he hollers back, " if you don't know, we're in a world of trouble!" So with the wind to my back and veering westerly of that, I visualize the chart again and try to reckon time lost and direction blown. Then I decide to veer more westerly still, so I make that correction. Because the shoal that Charlie hit has to mean that we are well beyond Wallace Channel and it's deeper waters and close to Shell Castle and it's shoaly waters. Then out of the steady rain one hundred yards ahead, like home sweet home suddenly found finally, come the high shell banks of Shell Castle that the pelicans like. So I holler, "there, Carl!", and point. And he looks and hollers, "damn if you don't have these waters down good, Keith!" So I smile real big because now I like myself a whole lot.

So now we are around and beyond Shell Castle to the south and west and where Carl and I had been Tuesday afternoon. But the astern wind is still trying to blow Charlie and Jack around and to the side of us, but I simply cannot give the outboard more throttle because our nosing in is already too bad now. So I decide that we have to come about into the wind now, even though I would prefer to be a little farther west, because this towing with the wind isn't working any longer and things could get real serious fast. So I holler to Carl, "we're going to snap them like popping a whip when we come about and go into the wind." And Carl thinks about that and hollers back, "I'll pull them up close to us, then you come about, then I'll feed out the line cushioning the shock." So I nod and say okay. Then Carl does and I do and he does, and it works! And Carl and I sigh a big sigh of relief. And Charlie and Jack look like they have gone beyond scared and are into numb and just holding on for dear life. But now all we have to do is beat against the wind for the not too far distance to the Bank creek and to shelter finally.

So the four of us give the bow of Charlie's skiff a hard push and the stern goes up high and dry on the sandy shore of the Bank creek. Then Charlie walks there and starts to see what it is going to take to get the right side of the stern reattached to the hull. But down here in the creek we are out of the wind, and that is a welcome change. But the rain is a constant downpour, and that is miserable still. And with our foul weather coats on with the hoods up, we look like a small gathering of monks here gathered around Charlie's skiff.

So Carl says, "fellas, we've got a problem."

And we look at him like, 'no shit Sherlock, tell us something we don't know.'

"Seriously," Carl says, "Charlie can get the stern reattached. But it may or may not hold for the beat back to Ocracoke. So Keith and I better take all the gear. But then we won't have room for the clams. That's the problem. "

So we start thinking about that   Start trying to deal with that. But we have already dealt with about as many problems as we can stand, here with this way too much way too soon all around us again. Be we must deal with this problem also.

So I say, "hell with the clams. We dump them where they are, then come back next week and get them. They won't go anywhere."

"Let me get back to Swansboro, and you'll never catch my ass up here again, and I mean that," Charlie says in a rush.

"Me too," Jack says. "You and Carl can have our clams. We owe y'all for the bail anyway."

"We each have about three hundred dollars worth," Charlie says, "but I could care less. Just let me get my ass back to Swansboro. "

"Me too," Jack says.

"Carl?" I ask.

"I'm not in the mood to come back here either, even if it is beautiful weather," Carl says, "but okay, I'll probably feel differently in a couple of days."

"Okay. But if y'all change your minds, we'll all come back," I say to Charlie and Jack.

"I won't change my mind. Just let me get my ass back to Swansboro, please" Charlie says.

"Me too," Jack says.

So Jack holds the bow of Charlies's skiff, and Charlie starts to work on the stern. And Carl and I go and start knocking down the camp and getting all the gear stowed in my skiff. By the time we have this done, Charlie has the twisted right hand bracket off and pounded out straight and uses it to attach the stern to the hull again. Then he tears a teeshirt in strips and with a screwdriver starts to caulk the teeshirt strips into the joint. And this should hold at least for the beat against the wind back to Ocracoke. So we all go and dump the clams where they are. And they will quickly bury themselves naturally in the sandy bottom of the creek and be none the worse for wear next week. Then we stuff many empty sacks into one empty sack, then put these stuffed sacks deep in the marsh grass so they will be here next week also. Then we give the entire area a final walk around to be sure we haven't forgotten anything and that all the trash is picked up.

And the beat against the wind back to Ocracoke is just that, simply one more long beat in a open skiff out in the middle of a whole lot of very unruly water, with the salt spray again stinging my eyes looking from under my hood and with my skiff again slamming and framming and rolling and pitching endlessly. With Carl and I standing holding the tight bowline and trying to maintain footing, but with us not talking because there just isn't anything to say. With us just silently enduring this long beat because this too will end eventually. Then there are the breakwater boulders. But we are too exhausted to get excited. They are just there and we accept it as that. But there aren't any Guardsmen looking as we pass the Station. So I think, 'maybe they feel responsible for prudent but unlucky sailors, but they stop feeling responsible for a bunch of idiots who insist upon playing out in a screaming northeaster for three days.' Then I think, 'naw, the Coast Guard wouldn't feel that way.'

Then things get frantic at the dock because the last ferry is getting ready to leave. So we quickly get all the gear divided and transferred to the trucks. Then we quickly get our skiffs hauled out and tied down securely. Then as Charlie and Jack start for the ferry landing, I go in to say goodbye to Luther Styron. And I quickly tell him what all happened today, and I finish with, "so my partner and I will be back next week for a couple of days to get the clams we left and a few more."

And during this he just smiles and shakes his head, sitting there one cheeked on the stool with his left leg still outstretched resting. Then he says, "you're a glutton for punishment all right, Keith."

"I really love it up here, Mr. Styron, but I'll love it even more next week when the weather is beautiful." And he says that he can certainly understand that and we shake hands and say goodbye.

So as soon as Carl and I drive on the ferry, the stern gate goes up and the big diesels start their heavy throbbing and the ferry begins to pull away from the landing. So that is cutting it close, too close in fact. But Cedar Island here we come now. Yes! But then it begins to get dark as it quickly goes from can see to can't see in a very few minutes. Then we feel the wind and the rain jolt the ferry when we get out beyond Ocracoke's lee shore. But today is the first day that the ferry has run since this mess started. And today was just a half schedule day. So we are lucky to be on it. Yes, lucky for a lot of reasons and lucky in a lot of ways. And suddenly I think how very good it is going to feel to be safe and warm and dry in my Swansboro apartment again. Yes!

So Carl asks, "what's today?"

"I don't know. Uh, Thursday. I think." And I try hard to think through my complete exhaustion. "Yeah, it's Thursday. I think."

"I feel like I've been whipped all over with a stick."

And I answer yeah me too.

"It'll take several days for me to get over this trip, that's for sure."

And I answer yeah me too.

So now it is full dark and the rain pelts and splatters the back glass of the truck, and the wind gusts around the truck shaking it. But we are out of it now. It
can't get to us now. Yes, we are out of it finally. So I ask, "want a beer?", as I reach to the ice cooler on the floorboard. And Carl answers, "hell yeah, if we haven't earned any other beer, we've earned this one." And I answer that's for sure, Carl.

Then in a few minutes Carl says that he will call Sara from the pay phone at the ferry landing to let her know that we are all right. And he says that when he talked to her last night she said that the storm wasn't too bad down there, that we must be getting the worst of it up here. So Carl and I laugh as we enthusiastically agree that yes we sure as hell did get the worst of it up here. And Carl says that he won't soon forget this trip. And I say yeah that someone should write a book about it. And we go on like this for awhile.

But it isn't long before we get quiet. Because with our exhaustion deepening, talking becomes just too much work. So we turn inward to our own thoughts. So I remember Jennifer for the first time in days. But strangely now she seems only like someone I use to know a long time ago in another place. But once again I simply refuse to let myself remember the shame of my using her so. Because I still have the rest of my life for doing that, and now isn't the right time for self-punishment. So I wonder where she is right now. Who the hell knows. San Francisco, New Orleans, who the hell knows.   And suddenly I realize that I really don't care where she is.   Suddenly, gone is the old anguish and torment of lost and gone Jennifer, and when oh when will she ever return. Somehow the emptiness of her absence does not hurt any longer. So I feel guilty as though I am somehow betraying the us that we were, and I blame it on all the recent excitement and on my exhaustion now.   But it isn't this, and I know it isn't this.   Then I know that something about she and I broke inside of me during the past several days, and that now it is different so I am different.   But I can't explain it to myself yet. But I know that this is so.

But I do still envy Carl's having Sara who cares whether he lives or dies.   Carl's having Sara to go home to.   Carl's having a fisherman's wife rather than just a wife.   But I don't envy who Carl has, I envy what Carl has that I don't have.   But it is a friendly envy and not a greedy envy.   Because Jennifer's comments when I tell her about this trip will be something like, "well, none of it sounds really necessary to me Keith, why put yourself through that when you could be getting the seafood market going and making something of yourself?"   Because she has never understood why it is so necessary for me to be not just a fisherman but a good fisherman, and she never will.   So I can explain to her the excitement and the danger and the challenge of this trip until the cows come home, and it will mean absolutely nothing to her because to her none of it is necessary in the first place.   And nothing or no one can change that about her.

But Jennifer can turn my crank like no woman ever has been

able to before, and like no woman ever will be able to again. Her husky voice, her perfume, her pouting mouth, her black black hair, all devastate me, they really do. And sex is a big part of it, but it isn't all of it. Maybe it is as simple as badly wanting something that you know you can never have, which makes you want it all the more. Maybe that is all it has ever been, and all it ever will be. So when she reappears in a week, a month, whenever, everything will be the same for the several days until she disappears again. But now I know that it is the hurt and the anguish and the torment that was recently broken, that will never come again. But whatever it is that she and I are together will gradually fade away when I move to Cedar Island, because then I no longer will be convenient to her. But that will be her decision to make and not my decision to make. Yeah, Carl is right, nothing about Jennifer and I is healthy, not healthy at all. So I cross my arms on my lap so my elbow scrapes aren't touching anything and I lean my head back on the seat, and to the steady throb of the ferry diesels and the pelt of the rain and the gust of the wind, I close my eyes so they won't sting as badly.

CHAPTER THIRTEEN

So the morning is drizzly and cool breezy and dreary, and I am weary, so everything fits. So it will be a throw away day, but that is okay by me. But the forecast is for this mess to finish blowing itself out tonight, then clear and warm tomorrow. Then the next day it will be back to the ninety ninety five days for awhile. But September isn't far now, yes, so the dog days are about over with for this summer thankfully because my too burnt skin badly needs some relief it certainly does. September and October and November are gorgeous and comfortable for working the water as bay fishermen. Just as April and May and June are gorgeous and comfortable also. So during spring and fall we store up the good memories of the really nice weather to remember during the summer and the winter when the harsh weather is brutal and we wonder why the hell we do what we do where we do it.

So early tomorrow morning I will sort through my camping gear and hang out most of it to dry. Then I will launch my skiff down at Casper's and go clamming for at least a short day because the fun and games will be over with and it will be time to get back to work, because I am just about broke what with the money spent for expenses and bail money but my clams are still at Shell Castle. Then the middle of next week Carl and I will go get the clams and we will stay for least one full work day plus the part days of the go and come days, so I should get back here with close to twelve hundred dollars and I will put a thousand of that on 'Secret Woman' as down payment. Then I will begin to get the thousand for the first year's payment. And to give that a boost, I have decided to make a trip to clam Shell Castle in mid September. But that trip I will make alone.

Because of all the things I have to learn during the next year, the most important thing is that I must learn to work the water alone. And that is an unsettling thought, scary even, but quite necessary if I am finally to become a bay fisherman. Because the few remaining real old time bay fishermen that we see working the water around here, go alone and work alone and come in alone. They are friendly and helpful and we often talk and several of them I know fairly well, but always they keep their own council and they work alone. It is us younger fishermen who discuss together and plan together and usually work with a partner somewhere close by. And that is a good way to learn and to gain experience. But once you have learned and have gained experience, and once you have acquired the necessary boats and gear to be versatile, then it is time for you to begin to keep your own council and to work alone. And that is what they really mean when they say, if you're man enough to take a boat away from the dock, you better be man enough to bring the boat back. Because then you have only yourself to depend upon and rightly so.

After all, Oscar Schneider worked 'Secret Woman' alone for all of the years he had her until he physically got so he simply could not work the water any longer. But for all those years he alone decided which fishery to fish and how to rig for it and when to start the season and when to stop the season. He alone decided whether to go and when to go and where to go and when to come in. And through it , Oscar always kept his own council and he worked alone. So now, Keith, it is your turn and it is your time. So I have decided to stay around here until late December. Because the fall shrimp season will last until then. So I will clam my skiff, and I will shrimp 'Secret Woman' around here until then. Then I will move to Cedar Island in early January. But January and February and March are the worst weather months, and the off season months for fish and shrimp, and therefore the leanest money months for a bay fisherman working the water. But those months are the bay scallop season months, so I will scallop 'Secret Woman' in Core Sound for the several days a week of that season. And the other days a week, I will pearake clam my skiff over around Chain Shot Island and Wainright Island and over behind Portsmouth Island. But I will lose a lot of days to bad weather. But I will endure. Then in spring, I will run 'Secret Woman' from Cedar Island across Pamlico Sound like the ferry does and return home again to clam Shell Castle. And in May the flounder season starts, so I will flounder 'Secret Woman' until fall. And I will keep my own council and I will work alone and I will endure.

So I go find Oscar sitting on the bench down at Casper's, out of the drizzle and breeze and leaning with both hands on his cane and looking far across the water, just where I figured he would be.

And he smiles big when I come up because he knew about the northeaster and he has been concerned. Just as many in Swansboro have been concerned because four of her clammers were up there caught out in it for three days in only skiffs. So Oscar and I shake hands and we say hello and I sit beside him on the bench. And he says y'all made it back okay and I say yeah a little worse for wear but we made it back okay and he says well that's the main thing. So right away I begin to rattle on in great detail all about the trip. And through it Oscar smiles and chuckles and shakes his head and thoroughly enjoys my long tale of blunder and danger and hardship, that I tell light heartedly because once the worst of it has passed fishermen minimize the danger and maximize the blunder. So that with each telling of the tale, the danger gradually diminishes until finally it is non existent, and the blunder is hugely expanded upon until finally it is unbelievable. Because that is what fishermen do.

Then I tell Oscar that I really do want 'Secret Woman', and I tell him my plans for how I will pay for her. And right away he is real happy, and he says my making the thousand down payment next week when Carl and I get back from Ocracoke is fine with him. And my making the first thousand yearly payment by late October, is fine, and we will worry about next year's payment next year and I say fine. Then I tell Oscar about Luther Styron and sundogs, and I say that I think I can learn a lot from Luther about all the weather signs and such and about fishing up there, so long as I don't pester him too much and make a habit of it, and Oscar nods his head yes.

Then I tell him all my plans for around here this fall, and my plans for the winter up around Cedar Island and Core Sound, and my plans for a spring and into summer out toward home at Shell Castle. And by now Oscar's gnarly old fisherman's hands are really shaking on his cane because he has gotten my excitement himself and he is living it right along with me because old fishermen dearly love it when young fishermen share their enthusiasm and their honest love of boats and fishing and the water.

Then when I finish we are both wide eyed with excitement and breathing hard. So we don't talk for a minute while we calm down. And for this minute we both just look through the drizzle and the cool breezes far across the water.

Then Oscar looks at me and gently says, "you're enjoying all this, aren't you Keith?"

And I think about that and say, "yes Oscar, I'm having the time of my life, I really am." And I really am, because all of this is one hell of an adventure. And Oscar smiles and nods because once he was there himself, when all the best fishing years were still ahead.

But I know that I am in for one terrible ragging from Wormshoe when I get to Sammy's. And sure enough, I no sooner walk in and Wormshoe breaks into a big grin and starts, "so how's your asshole puckering now, smart ass!"

So I get a surprised look on my face and say, "what do you mean, Wormshoe, what are you talking about?"

And he scoffs, "come off it, Keith, Carl was just in and told me all about it. I told you, didn't I tell you, the Pamlico Sound will get you if you don't watch out."

"Just a little wind, a little rain, nothing to it, Wormshoe."

"Come off it, admit it Keith, you were scared shitless."

So I admit it, "well, it did get pretty hairy there a couple of times ."

"I told you so, didn't I tell you so?"

So I admit that also.

"Well, glad you're back safe." He says through the still big grin, and I can tell by his now glistening eyes that he really is. "I bought Carl a beer, now I'm buying you one," and he slides the beer across the bar. "Shake," he says, and he reaches out his hand and we shake.

"Thanks Wormshoe, it's good to be back," and it is, it really its.

So I go play the poker hand slot machine, and right away I win thirty dollars. So I say to it, "now I'm finally through with you you bitch. Swore that if I ever got back close to even, I'd be through with you, now I am." And I am. So I go back and sit at the bar and watch Wormshoe fill one end of the beer cooler. Then I remember Larry, so I look but he isn't at the bar or among the crowd playing pool. "Where's Larry, Wormshoe?"

"He's gone."

"He usually doesn't go home this early."

"No, he's gone. Gone to Georgia."

"Georgia? What the hell for?"

"Don't know," Wormshoe shrugs and says, "he came in Monday afternoon, and said he was leaving Tuesday morning. Said it was time for him to move on. Said he wanted to get settled in before fall. Said the cold isn't as bad down there, and cold bothers him a lot more now."

"Well I be damned. Didn't even say goodbye."

"He stored some stuff in back. Said he'd be back for it in a month or so. You'll probably see him then." Then Wormshoe gets back to filling that end of the cooler.

"Well I'll be damned," I say outloud to myself, looking at my much too tanned face in the long bar mirror. And suddenly I really miss the aggravating, cantankerous, one way old fart. So I think, 'and the old fart didn't even say goodbye,' like my feelings are hurt. But this never was the all of us in it together that I tried to make it. We never were all at camp and sitting around a campfire at sunset and singing camp songs like I tried to make it. We were just a gathering of fellas from all over who decided to work the water around here as bay fishermen for these years. Some better at it than the others. Some more serious about it than the others. But it couldn't last and it couldn't stay the same. And it never was supposed to. Because we each came here alone with our lives, and we will each leave here alone with our lives. And that is how it's supposed to be. And that is how it is. After all, aren't you soon going to Cedar Island alone? So I gently lean my forearms on the bar so my elbow scrapes aren't touching and continue looking at my much too weathered self in the mirror and say outloud to myself, "yeah, that's how it's supposed to be all right," like I am rough and tough and can handle anything. But suddenly I feel very lonely and very uncertain about everything. Because up there is over fished just like down here is over fished. So all I'll be doing is changing places but nothing will be different. And I won't know anyone up there, but I have many friends down here. So I'll wrestle inside with that for a minute before deciding that it just can't be helped, that it is just part of it. Because just like Larry, I know it is time now for me to move on. But at least the pollution isn't to up there yet like it is to down here. Yeah, but it is getting to up there very quickly because all the rivers that flow into the Pamlico Sound are already dead which is a truly staggering fact. So all those hundreds of square miles of estuary and habitat are already polluted to death and gone. And the whole huge Pamlico Sound itself is next. Then the whole simply gigantic Atlantic Ocean itself is next. Because what is happening here in North Carolina is happening everywhere. And I will see these devastating deaths in my lifetime. Then what? Then we will have killed ourselves just like Portsmouth City killed itself so many years ago. Because mother nature simply will not be screwed with. And her payback is terrible indeed. But I'm a fisherman not a politician . No, but maybe you had better learn to be one along with learning to be a fisherman and whatever else. Well damn if you aren't staking out a real big chunk of things for you to learn to be in however many years you have left. Yeah, well that's what all this has really been about. It's been about getting good at things, and taking things seriously, and it's been about getting involved. Because after all, who knows better than fishermen how all this fits together out here.

Then Tom comes in and sits on the stool beside me, and Wormshoe brings us beer, and I'm real glad to have someone to talk with so I'll get out of the doomsday mood. So right away Tom starts talking about boat building, because that is about all he has on his mind these days. So we sit here and build boats for awhile. And I am impressed with how far Tom has come with it since he started only several months ago. Then in a lull I tell him that I am going to buy the 'Secret Woman', and he says, "good move, Keith, fine trawler, mighty fine trawler." And he says that he will be glad to help me with anything that might need fixing. So I thank him then I start asking him about the care and maintenance of the three fifty Chevrolet engine that is in her. Because I will have to learn to be an engine mechanic also.

Then later my apartment is hushed with the night sounds of solitude again. I am standing at the living room window looking down the grassy slope to the tall yard lights and Casper's and the docked boats and beyond to the red and green channel marker lights of the Waterway that go into the darkness. The drizzle has just about ended and now and then I can see the quarter moon where the clouds are broken. So this mess is clearing out finally. So I remember Jennifer and I standing here a week ago tonight with one arm around each other's waist as we watched the well lighted tug pushing the darkened barge, then our slow soft kiss. But that is as far as I let myself think about Jennifer. Because what's the use? Because what difference would it make anyway? So I remember how happy and how tired Billie Griffin looked when we were coming back from clamming a week ago tomorrow. Has it only been a week, but it seems a lifetime ago, yes? We were coming back slowly in my skiff from the clam buyer's and Billie was holding her twelve dollars for the day in both her hands tenderly and she looked really precious in the rag dolly clothes and the floppy hat as she looked for the last time across the mudflats and the winding creeks and the marsh islands to the backside dunes of Bear Island. And I thought then, 'how quickly she could become one of us,' and I still think so standing here now. So I think, 'hell, give her a call, it would be great talking with her, and maybe she could come down for a weekend sometime soon.' So now I am smiling, and suddenly I feel real good about things. So I think, 'hell, that's a good idea, why didn't you think of it before? Well, it's been a busy week, remember? Yes I do, yes hell it has. But everything is changed and different now, and all in only a week!' So I go to the phone and dial Charlotte information and get her number. Then I dial it and when she answers I say, "Billie, this is Keith Englund in Swansboro."

"Keith, what a wonderful surprise!" and she does sound surprised, but then she sounds concerned, "is anything wrong?"

"No, just felt like calling and talking with you."

"Well, what a wonderful surprise. Keith, clamming with you last Saturday was one of the best days I've ever had. And I really mean that. I told my science class all about it Monday. They even got excited. What a wonderful day, Keith, and I appreciate your taking me."

"Well, I was thinking that maybe you could come down for a weekend sometime soon. We could take my skiff to Cedar Island and launch it and ride around up there. It is very beautiful up there, Billie, it really is"

"Gosh Keith, I don't know when Jennifer and Robert will be down there again for me to stay with."

"No, I mean you come down, I could get you a motel room. Maybe you could bring your son, he would really enjoy it."

But now Billie doesn't say anything for almost a minute. Then she says, "Keith, Jennifer and I have been friends since college. I wouldn't feel right doing that."

"Oh, yeah, okay, well, just thought I'd ask." But I had forgotten all about Jennifer. So now I feel very foolish because now I realize that this was a bad idea.

"Keith, I'm flattered, really, but Jennifer and I have been friends since college. If it wasn't for that." Then her voice trails off.

"Look, you're right, I wasn't thinking, Billie, I'm sorry. It was a stupid idea, I guess, but." But then my voice trails off also.

"Maybe we can do it when Jennifer and Robert are down again."

"Sure, that sounds good, Billie. Sure, maybe we can."

Then she says okay great but then neither of us knows what to say so finally we stutter and grope our way to saying goodbye. So I hang up the phone and sit here in the red plaid chair and say outloud to myself, "well dumb ass, that wasn't one of your better ideas, was it?"

So I go stand looking out of the window into the broken cloud night again. But I had completely forgotten about Jennifer. I really had. Because everything is changed and different now, so I had completely forgotten about her. But what a terrible position to put Billie in. So I say, "damn Keith, sometimes you can be so stupid." Yeah but Billie didn't say, how dare you, and don't you ever call me again. No, she didn't say that. Okay then. So how about if you call her next week and tell her about buying 'Secret Woman,' and just talk about that. Then the next week call and tell her about your going back to Shell Castle, but this time you're going alone. Then the following week tell her about your plans to shrimp around here this fall, then move to Cedar Island in January. And keep the conversations light and cheerful and positive. And soon she will begin to look forward to your calls, and soon she will begin to expect your calls. And gradually she will come to understand that things really are changed and different now. Yeah, that just might work. Yeah, I bet that will work. And we will name our first son Oscar, and we will name our second son Luther. And our first daughter of course we will name Lola.